Diary Of An
Almost Cool Girl

Books 1 to 3

Meet Maddi...Ooops!
My New School
Meet The Cousins

B. Campbell

D1280157

Dedication

Diary of an Almost Cool Girl is dedicated to the hundreds of "almost cool girls" I have taught over the years.
You are all very special! Don't ever let anyone tell you otherwise!
Thank you for giving me heaps of funny things to write about.

Table of Contents

Story 1 - Meet Maddi – Ooops!

Where it all began…

The shrill sound of sirens vibrated the frame of the window
I'm looking through. Up here on the second level of my
school, I have a good view of the science block. Although the
smoke haze is still lazily drifting from the windows that
were smashed so the firemen could put their hoses in.
Within a minute, they called out that the fire was under
control.

I personally think the second fire unit and the two ambulances were a bit over the top. Nobody got hurt and the fire was only in the waste paper basket.

I've been sitting in the Principal's office now for about 15 minutes, waiting for my mom to arrive so that the Principal can inform her about, "How Madonna Bull tried to burn the school down."

They are his words – not mine.

How did I end up in the Principal's office, you ask. Well let me explain, it's all in my diary.

Monday

Hi everyone, welcome to my diary. Some people write their diaries as private memories for themselves, me…I'm different, I like to write it for an audience. My name is Madonna Bull, most people call me Maddi.

Some kids call me Mad or even Mad Bull, but I just ignore those types of kids. I'm not one of the "cool" kids and I'm not none of the "brainy" kids…I'm just a normal girl. Sometimes I like to think of myself as an "almost cool girl". Not in the "cool" group, but I'm not a nerd either.

I'm 12, well nearly 12. Okay, I'm 11 years, six months and 3 days to be exact.

I must confess, I have a bad habit. I like to give people nicknames, but don't panic, I don't call anyone by their nicknames, I just use them in my diary. So I guess only you and me know about them.

For example, my mom is an alternative hippy type mom, carefree and always looking on the bright side of things. Like when I dropped two dinner plates and they both broke, Mom just comes out with, "That's okay, Madonna, it just means less washing up to do."

And that is why her nickname is Mrs. Absolutely Positive. She is positive and enthusiastic about EVERYTHING! Mom also loves exercise, yoga and healthy food. She is really into those yucky green drinks with vegetables in them…gross!

Dad is big with a loud booming voice, so his nickname is Mr. Boom Boom. I wonder what my nickname for you would be if I knew you.

I blame my parents for the "nickname" thing. They give everyone in our neighborhood a nickname. Sometimes it is a bit embarrassing because we don't remember their real names. Labrador man (yes he walks a Labrador dog) and Bob (not his real name, but he is a builder – like in Bob the Builder) all live close by. So using nicknames is a family tradition that I have inherited.

My parents have given me some shocking nicknames. The first one was Poo Shooter because of my ability to shoot explosive poos across the room...when I was a baby.

When I got a bit older, around 6, they called me Princess Grotty Snotty, due to an unfortunate incident when I was wearing my best princess costume. I had a cold and my nose was full of thick gooey green snot.

Mom had taken me to the shopping center to go to the doctors and on the way out was taking a short cut through the food court. That's where it all went terribly wrong. Halfway through the eating area, a dear old granny type lady said to my mom, "What a beautiful princess you have there," – that's me of course. Granny lady stops eating her lovely looking cake and starts telling me how pretty I look. You know how, when you have a cold, you have no control over when your body decides to sneeze...well my body decided to sneeze just as she finished those kind words and smiled at me. Not just any sneeze, but perhaps the biggest and greatest sneeze in the history of mankind. Ahhhhh Chooooo!!!!

That stopped granny lady in her tracks. She looked down at her yummy cake and it is covered in two rivers of snot. She claps her hands across her mouth. Making retching sounds she races from her table towards the toilets. Meanwhile, mom grabs my hand and drags me off to the car. Being Mrs. Absolutely Positive she says, "It's okay, Maddi, better out than in. And besides, that cake was so unhealthy, she would have been much better off eating some nice fresh fruit." Did I mention that Mom is really into healthy food?

And that is how I collected the lovely nickname of Princess Grotty Snotty.

Anyway, enough diary for today. I need to do my homework and so probably do you.

Tuesday

My best friend Shelby and I walked to school this morning.
We have been friends for a long time now, since about
halfway through last year. I'm pretty quiet and try to avoid
being the center of attention while Shelby is the opposite.
She is loud and outgoing and loves being in the spotlight.
Mom says we get along so well because we balance each
other out. She said something about yin and yang, but I have
no idea what she is talking about.

Today when we were in Music class we were sitting together
as always. Mr. Canary (not his real name, just a great
nickname, loves to sing his instructions to us), asked us to sit
on the floor in a circle. Mr. Canary clapped out a rhythmic
pattern and we each in turn had to copy his pattern. Of
course the pattern changed for each student. Music is not my
strong point, even when trying to clap the beat to a song, I'm
likely to miss my own hands altogether. Obviously I'm not
the only one feeling the pressure...as everyone is absolutely
quiet as we await our turns.

There is a pause after each time Mr. Canary demonstrates a
clapping pattern and in those few seconds you could hear a
pin drop. It's nearly our turn, I can see Shelby is nervous as
she keeps fidgeting. I'm so glad she is before me as it gives
me a little more time. If you get the clapping pattern correct,
Mr. Canary gives you a treat. So as well as not wanting to
embarrass myself, I also really want a treat!

Mr. Canary claps out the rhythm for the girl sitting next to
Shelby and the silence before the girl starts her turn seems
absolute. Until an eardrum bursting fart noise rips across the
room. I can even feel the vibration on the wooden floor and
instantly realize that Shelby is the source of the noise. Poor
Shelby! I feel embarrassed for her, so I try to think of

something to say to ease her embarrassment.

No need – Shelby's next comment solves the problem. "Oh Maddi, that smells terrible!"

"I'm sorry Sir, Maddi has been suffering diarrhea, I'll just take her to the toilet and make sure she is okay." Then Shelby rustles me out of the classroom door as the laughter from the rest of the class drowns out my protests of innocence.

Once outside Shelby breaks into hysterical laughter, humiliating me even more.

But in the end I just give up and join in the laughter.

Eventually Shelby says, "Well, Maddi, I may have ruined your image, but at least I got us out of clapping those stupid patterns."

Thursday

Despite the odd embarrassing moment, I'm lucky to have a good friend like Shelby. Having friends is especially important when you have a Bethany Barker in your class. Bethany is the mean girl of our school, some kids love sport, some love achieving A's, some love the arts, but Bethany just loves being mean. That's right folks, a genuine bully in my class.

Generally I don't have too much trouble with her. Shelby and I are nearly always together and Shelby is simply too loud to pick on. I've already told Bethany – whom I secretly call MG (short for mean girl) that I don't really care about her opinion.

One day MG must have been low on her quota of kids to pick on, when she came across Shelby and I in the playground. MG started making negative and nasty comments about my appearance. Like all bullies, MG always seemed to have a little band of followers. Sarah and Sue (who must be very desperate for friends to hand out with MG) were with MG. As usual, MG would make the nasty remarks and her followers, Sarah and Sue, would laugh at her "amazing" wit.

Mom always taught me the best way to deal with bullies is to ignore them or stand-up to them. I decided to try a bit of both. First I just totally ignored MG's nasty comments and I kept talking to Shelby.

After about 5 minutes of ignoring MG's little rant, I saw Shelby's face begin to show her anger at her friend being insulted. I put my hand softly on her shoulder and said, "It's okay, I'll handle this."

I turned to MG and calmly said, "Thanks Bethany, I'm always ready to accept constructive criticism about my appearance from intelligent, fashionable and thoughtful people like yourself."

Bethany looked confused.

Then I continued in a calm and confident voice, "But hang on, I just realized, you're definitely not intelligent, nor thoughtful and perhaps not even fashionable, so I really couldn't care less about your opinion."

Shelby burst into laughter, even one of MG's cronies had a little chuckle.

I led Shelby away as MG growled at her friends for laughing.

Friday

Today during the lunch break, MG was picking on Caroline. Caroline is only new to my school and tends to keep to herself. At first we didn't realize what was happening, but as soon as we did, Shelby and I sat on either side of her.

"Bye Bethany," says Shelby in her best "I'm not scared of you" tone of voice. Ever since our last run in with Bethany, she has avoided us – which we love! Bethany shrugs her shoulders, pokes her tongue out and stomps off in a huff.

That's when we see the tears in Caroline's eyes. She reveals to us that MG has been bullying her almost every day since she arrived at our school. MG has been quietly calling her names in class. So quiet that the teacher and other kids can't hear. And she has been pushing her books off the table as she walks past Caroline's desk.

We tell Caroline that she should tell the teacher what is happening, but apparently MG told Caroline that the teachers at our school hate kids who tell on other kids and that the teachers will only tell her to "just deal with it".

Shelby and I are horrified, I explain to Caroline that bullies often make up stories like this to stop their victims from getting help. "Our teachers are great! If you tell them about Bethany, they'll do their best to stop her," I explained.

Monday

In the morning, Caroline told us that she had taken our
advice and spoken to her favorite teacher, Miss Jenkins. At
about 9:30 the principal came into the classroom and took
Caroline away for about an hour.

Then when he returned with Caroline, he took MG away
with him. She walked back into the classroom about 40
minutes later. MG's shoulders were slumped as she quietly
returned to her seat. It looked like she had been crying.

At first break, MG kept well away from Caroline. She sat
and ate her apple and didn't strut around looking for
victims, like she does every other break.

Caroline told us that the principal (I call him Mr. Sausage
Nose – he has a really long nose) wanted to know everything
that MG had done. She said he was great and he assured her
that he would speak to Bethany and that Caroline should
come directly to him if she bothered her anymore. Caroline
was so happy and couldn't stop thanking us for giving her
the courage to speak up. Hi-5's all around.

Bullies 0 – Almost Cool Girls 1!

Tuesday

Mathematics today was so boring! Mr. Wettan or as I like to call him, Mr. Facebook…was at his worst. Unfortunately I have him for both Math and Science, so he is double trouble and doubly bad!

Mr. Facebook (can you guess why?) is only a young teacher. He always has his phone on his desk with Facebook open.

Today he started out with a lesson on fractions and this lesson was starting to look interesting, when his phone made a quiet ding sound. You know the type of noise that lets you know when someone has posted something on your wall. Mid-sentence, Mr. Facebook stops talking and rushes over to his phone. He has a quiet chuckle to himself and suddenly realizes the whole class is sitting there watching him.

He quickly brings up a Math video on the data projector and instructs us to watch it. Then he sits at his desk and taps out messages on his phone for the rest of the lesson.

The video was really boring! The best part was when the principal walked in. Mr. Facebook jumped out of his chair like a startled rabbit! That phone disappeared so fast into his pocket that he may have set a new "hide the phone, speed record".
I think the principal may have seen it. They had a short conversation and although I couldn't make out the words, the tone of voice from the principal didn't sound very happy. When the principal left, the phone stayed in Mr. Facebook's pocket. It was funny because every couple of minutes we could see it vibrating.

Wednesday

The day I've been dreading has finally arrived. I did my best to avoid it! I tried to hide those notes in the bottom of my school bag. I deleted those online school newsletters as soon as I could from our home computer. I even tried to fake being too sick to go to school today, but all that got me was a big spoon of apple cider vinegar, yuck!!!!! Seriously…do normal kids with normal parents have to gulp down that foul tasting vinegar? Uugghh! I'm sure that one day it will turn me into a full-blown zombie!

Sadly, all my best efforts have failed and today Mom is coming to school with me. She is volunteering in the school canteen for a day. Now I love my Mom…it's just when it comes to food she is VERY alternative. We eat enough salads to feed the vast grazing herds of Africa! Mom's idea of junk food is dipping your carrot stick into yoghurt. If it wasn't for Dad, I wouldn't even know about sugar or chocolate.

Our school canteen sells what they call a balanced menu. That means some healthy foods (by normal standards) and some less healthy foods – the really yummy stuff. So I'm a bit worried about how Mom will cope having to serve up food that goes against her healthy food values.

Once at school, Mom puts on her school canteen apron and bids me goodbye, with a cheery, "Be the best you can be, Madonna." That's my Mom, Mrs. Absolutely Positive.

I should have realized something was wrong when I kept getting odd looks as some of my classmates arrived in our room, after putting in their canteen orders.

Lunchtime revealed the full extent of my problem when a group of about ten students approached me as I sat next to Shelby and we began eating our lunch. Tiny (my nickname for David Burrows – the class football hero – who was actually a giant!) stood in front of me. "Maddi, is that your mother in the canteen? The one who is ruining all our lunches!"

"Well," I mumbled, "my mom is in the canteen, she is quite a good cook, I don't think she would RUIN anyone's lunch."

Then the whole group started yelling out their complaints in a storm of jumbled words.

"She made me have brown bread!"

"My ham and salad roll had NO ham!"

"My hotdog had tofu instead of a sausage!"

"I ordered a bag of chips and I got carrot and celery sticks!"

"She scraped all the icing off my cake and said there was enough sugar in the cake!"

"And I wanted a chocolate milkshake and she gave me a green smoothie, gross!!!! It looked like snot!"

This required some quick thinking! I smiled, "Well the good news is that you are all looking a lot healthier and Mom is only working in the canteen once a week for the rest of the term."

All the junk and fatty food fans started groaning and Shelby and I quickly made out escape towards the playground.

I didn't even bother discussing the canteen complaints with mom that night. I know what her response would be and I don't feel like a food lecture. Besides, I have to eat healthy food every day…it won't hurt them to have it once a week!

Saturday

What a day! Mom had invited her friend Demi over for lunch. Demi is an artist and while Mom is a bit of a hippy, Demi is an extreme "free spirit" type of person. Her daughter's name is Star and she is a year older than me. Star doesn't go to school, she is home-schooled. Don't get me wrong, I have nothing against home schooling, in fact I actually think home schooling would be great, but I think Star's education would be very different to my school. Math would probably involve a visit to the local hippy store and adding up the prices of all the weirdo hats. History would probably be watching an old movie. And Science would be gazing at the stars when night falls. Actually, it sounds pretty good!

Anyway I discovered Demi and mom talking in the kitchen as they prepared lunch. Demi greeted me with a cheery, "Hi Maddi, wow, your aura is looking so bright and happy." Then without touching me, she ran her hands around my body, "Your energy levels are magnificent, but I will have to talk to your mom about getting some crystal jewelry to protect you from bad energy."

Mom could see that I'm feeling a bit uncomfortable with all this attention. She breaks in, "Maddi, Star is in your room, you should go and say hi."

My mind races! Star is in my room. Who said she could go in there? My room is full of my private stuff. I race down to save my privacy.

TOO LATE!!!!!

Star is laying on my bed reading my diary! She looks over the top of the book as I burst into my room. Before she even says, "Hi Maddi," I rip my diary from her hands. She tries to snatch it back, "Come on Maddi, it was just getting interesting!"

Star is an imposing sight, tall for her age with her dyed jet black hair long on one side and almost shaved on the other side. She has multiple earrings and a fake tattoo on her arm (at least I think it is fake) and a stud in both of her eyebrows. I clutch my diary to my chest and screech, "How dare you read my diary, it's private!"

"Not anymore," she responds with a smirk. "Don't worry Maddi, I'm not interested in your dull little school dramas, my life is much more interesting," snarled Star.

At that moment Mom arrived, "Come on girls, we are going for lunch." Good timing Mom, Star and I were about to have our own version of wrestle mania.

On the trip to lunch, Mom and Demi chatted constantly, while Star and I sat in the back seat – in total silence!

In the restaurant, things continued much the same, until in a moment of unexpected meanness, Star tips her glass of juice into my lap. I squeal as the cold liquid hits my thighs. Finally Mom and Demi stop talking. They both grab some napkins and start to try and soak up the mess. The waiter comes over too and helps clean up the juice. He even replaces Star's drink.

Star keeps saying that she is sorry. I know she doesn't mean it. Mom says, "Don't worry dear, accidents happen." Star gives me her best fake smile and winks at me. I feel like tipping my juice over Star's head but show some restraint and decide to wait for a better chance for revenge.

The meals arrive, Star and I both have nachos with little side dishes of sour cream and chilli sauce. The chilli sauce is in a bottle that looks like a soda bottle. Star announces that she needs to go to the bathroom and I see my chance. As the waiter goes past I ask if I can I swap my chilli sauce for extra hot chilli sauce. I think he feels sorry for me and rushes off to change the sauce bottles. I quickly swap it with the bottle next to Star's plate.

Star returns and grabs the extra hot sauce bottle and dumps the whole lot over her nachos. She must be hungry, as she quickly scoffs two large mouthfuls of food into her mouth. Suddenly her eyes widen and she starts to cough. I guess that the extra hot chilli sauce is starting to take effect. While she is distracted I hand her the second bottle of chilli sauce, she thinks it is her soft drink and takes a large gulp. Her eyes bulge like some type of wild cartoon character and she explodes. A mouthful of sauce and nachos flies across the table. A bit hits Mom, but most of it splashes onto Demi. Needless to say, after that, lunch is over.

The ride home is pretty quiet, except for me munching my nachos and Star's occasional coughing and whimpering that her mouth is on fire. The waiter put my nachos in a take-away container and with a wink said, "Careful with that sauce."

Demi and Star head off in their car as soon as we got home. Mom gave me a stern look and asked if I had anything to do with what happened at lunch. I just smiled and replied, "I think those nachos had a dash of karma." Mom screwed up her face, trying to work out what I had meant. Then she shrugged her shoulders, gave me a kiss and went downstairs.

Monday

D is for disaster!
D is also for devastated!

Today after school the worst thing ever happened. Mom called me into the kitchen, Dad was already sitting at the breakfast table. Dad's normal happy smiling face had disappeared, replaced by a very sad mask. A glance at Mom revealed that her expression closely matched Dad's.

A million things raced through my mind!
Had they discovered I changed a C in Math on my last report card into a B with skillful use of a fine black marker?

Could it be that zombies are real and we are the last humans left?

Or, was I adopted and today I was to be returned to my rightful parents…the King and Queen of some European country?

Wrong!!!!!
Much worse!!!!!!

Mom and Dad haven't been getting along very well for the last few months and they have decided to separate for a while. There were tears all round, but Mom and Dad assured me they both still love me and we would still be a family, although Dad would be going away for a while.

I felt sad when Dad left that night, as did Mom. We cried on each other's shoulders. Dad had promised to contact us each day and Mom said she believed Dad would be back. She said it was the stress of his job causing him to be sad. True to his word, Dad calls or emails us every day and I just hope we'll all be back together one day.

I don't want to say…D is for divorce!

2 Weeks Later...
Tuesday

I haven't written in my diary for a while. I've been missing
Dad and so has Mom, so I've spent more time keeping her
company. For a while Mrs. Absolutely Positive lost her shine
and sparkle, but we have both settled down now. Dad still
contacts us every day and even though he isn't here, he is
still part of my life.

The funniest thing happened at school today in Math. My
History teacher's nickname is Mr. Oscar...because he is
always super grumpy! He reminds me of Oscar the grouch
from Sesame Street. He even has those big googly eyes
behind his glasses, just like the Oscar puppet.

Anyway, in his normal grouchy way he made everyone shift their seats so we weren't sitting with our friends. I ended up sitting between Bethany Barker (MG – short for mean girl) and a boy called Justin Smithers. I haven't had a lot to do with Justin, but have heard some of the "less kind" boys call him "Dustbin" rather than Justin.

That unfortunate name goes back to last year in my English class. Our teacher was a very young and pretty lady who was always beautifully dressed with perfect make-up and hair. So obviously I called her Miss Barbie!

Miss Barbie was quite a good teacher but was rather obsessed with neatness and cleanliness. Sometimes she would stop in the middle of a lesson to straighten the pencils and books on a kid's desk. She even had a bottle of hand sanitizer on her desk that she used every time after she touched our work books.

After lunch and playtimes she would spray an air freshener around the room. And she would always say the same thing, "We really don't want to be smelling all those sweaty bodies and foot odors all afternoon, do we children?"

Sometimes on particularly hot days she would tip some of her perfume onto a tissue and hold it up to her nose to protect her delicate senses from her foul-smelling students. So you get the picture…Miss Barbie is one delicate princess!

In her classroom the desks are always perfectly arranged in groups of six. One day as Miss Barbie moved around the room, I saw her nose begin to twitch and then her perfect face transformed into a grimace. With a puzzled look she slowly moved around the room, stopping at each desk and sniffing gently. "Does someone need to go to the bathroom?" she asks in her delicate sweet voice. She obviously thinks one of us has let off a smelly fart. Naturally nobody responded. Everyone put their heads down and focused on their work. Miss Barbie continued to sniff around the room.

"There is a really bad smell in here somewhere," she announced loudly with her sweet voice turning shrill as her delicate senses are assaulted by the smell. This time a few kids responded that they can smell something bad too. Miss Barbie starts a more intensive sniffing campaign, moving from one group to another.

Finally she returned to the group next to mine. In that group are 3 girls and 3 boys, one of the boys is Justin Smithers. She calls each of the kids out to the front of the class, one at a time, for a whispered conversation. I manage to just hear the words, "Are you sure you don't need to use the bathroom," as she talks to each of the kids. Miss Barbie does another circuit of the room before returning to the same group.

This time she starts going around the group instructing each student to open their desk. Miss Barbie has a quick look and a big sniff and then moves onto the next desk. She's found nothing so far and there are only two kids left, Justin and another boy.

Following Miss Barbie's instructions, Justin opens his desk wide and Miss Barbie takes a big sniff. She recoils in horror and takes two steps back. Her perfect face is pinched up into a scowl. She holds her nose as she uses a ruler to poke around in Justin's desk. With the tips of her fingers she lifts a plastic wrapped item from the desk, it oozes and drips and a disgusting stench floods the room.

Miss Barbie runs from the room, still clutching the stinking mess in her hand and making retching noises as she leaves.

Five minutes later, Mr. Sausage Nose – the principal, walks in and announces he will be taking the class as Miss Barbie has gone home sick.

After class the kids are giving Justin a bit of a hard time for causing the stink. He explains that he hadn't finished his hot dog at lunchtime so he had hidden it in his desk, intending to eat it in class while the teacher wasn't looking.

It could not have stunk that bad…just from lunchtime. We saw that it was starting to decompose, turning to mush!

Justin's mouth opened wide, he went white, "Oh no, it wasn't my hot dog from today, it was a hamburger from about 3 months ago! I forgot about it."

Apparently Justin couldn't smell it because he had his nose broken twice playing football and the injury had totally destroyed his sense of smell. And that is unfortunately how Justin got to be called Dustbin by some of our nastier class members.

Anyway, here I sit between Justin and Mean Girl, as Mr. Oscar fires lightning fast questions around the room. I follow the standard "avoid being picked to answer questions" tactics, appearing to listen intently and making no eye contact with the teacher and nodding wisely when someone else answered correctly.

When suddenly Mean Girl jabs me in the ribs with her sharp and boney elbow. I give an involuntary "oomph" as I double over in pain and surprise. That's when I make my mistake, I panic and look up to see if Mr. Oscar has heard me. Bad mistake! Our eyes lock! EYE CONTACT! Oh no....

"Right Maddi, next question is yours," snaps Mr. Oscar. Panic overtakes me, my pulse is beating faster than a speeding bullet. Here comes the question, I hold my breath, trying to focus. "What is the bluzen dinky xyt24 62536477flmkjqu," he asks. At least that is what it sounded like to me.

My... "I don't know" response gets a swift reaction. "I'll see you at lunchtime for some extra work, Maddi."

I steal a glance at Mean Girl and she gives me a self-satisfied smirk while poking her tongue at me.

31

Justin asks for a loan of a blue coloring pencil and I hand it over with a smile. As I work on my assignment, I notice that Justin is using my pencil for NON-coloring purposes. First he uses the non-sharpened end to give both his ears a good clean out, then he does a bit of exploration of his right nostril. It's hard to be sure but I think I see a little green thing on the end of my pencil.

Justin returns my pencil with a "thanks".

I reply, "Pop it on my desk." After a while I 'accidently' knock the pencil off my desk onto the floor. I don't want to hurt Justin's feelings, but there is NO WAY that I am going to put my fingers on that germ-covered pencil ever again!

The cleaners can have that one, they wear gloves when they pick up stuff from the classroom floor, so I know they won't catch anything.

Mean Girl must have seen me drop the pencil off my desk because she suddenly swoops down and picks it up. Why at this precise moment in world history does Mean Girl decide to be nice to me? I'm wracking my brain to think of reasons why I don't want the pencil back…without revealing the truth. If she knew why I didn't want the pencil back, she might use that information to tease Justin.

No need to worry! Mean Girl waggles the pencil at me and sneers, "Was this yours? Well not anymore, this is my favorite color."

As well as being a bully and a generally unlikeable person…Mean Girl has another off-putting habit. She chews on things – her fingers, her ruler, the ends of her hair and today she has something else to chew on…the end of my pencil.

GROSS! She has a good chew and I can't help but snigger. She hears me and turns and sticks even more of my pencil into her mouth to chew on. I laugh even more. A confused look shows on Mean Girl's face, me laughing was not the reaction she expected.

I decide not to tell her why I am laughing, not today…maybe another time when she is being a bully. It's so funny that I even manage to get through my lunchtime detention with a smile on my face.

Thursday

Science is looking interesting today. Mr. Facebook is taking our lesson in the actual science lab! There are beakers and test tubes and Bunsen burners and bottles of chemicals labeled with A, B, C and D on each of the tables.

Naturally Shelby and I grab a table together. Our table is at the far back corner of the room near a window. Unfortunately, it is a bit hard to hear Mr. Facebook from our table as he is demonstrating what to do from the front of the room.

Mr. Facebook is on fire (well not really on fire) and teaching a great lesson. He has us mixing chemicals and stuff and creating all kinds of exciting reactions like clouds of colored steam and popping bubbles bursting out of beakers.

The whole class is really involved and having fun. To be honest, we are all being a bit too noisy because the activities are so exciting.

Mr. Facebook announces that our last activity can be a little dangerous and to listen and watch carefully. He starts giving instructions on how to measure out quantities of different chemicals.

In our far corner, Shelby and I are struggling to hear his instructions. When he measured chemical C…we couldn't tell if he said 15mls or 50mls. So I went to the front to ask him. Just as I got there, he pulled out his phone, obviously he had heard a Facebook notification. "Excuse me," I asked politely, "did you say 15 or 50?" His attention is firmly fixed on his phone now and he answers, "Yes" to my question. Even I know that "yes" isn't the right answer. I repeat the question.

Mr. Facebook is now typing away on his phone and if possible...giving me even less attention. "50!" he snarls, followed by, "get back to your table and do your experiment."

I go back to the table and tell Shelby he said 50. She looks doubtful but what can we do? We start to combine our chemicals into the one large beaker. First chemical A and then chemical B. We hesitate as nothing has happened. The group at the next table have just finished pouring in chemical C. From their beaker we see a puff of smoke and hear a loud pop.

That doesn't look too scary, so I grab the 50ml of chemical C that we have already measured out and pour it into the beaker (containing the other chemicals). I'm holding the beaker in my left hand, watching it closely. I can see the mixture of chemicals bubbling up, heading towards the top of the beaker. If the group next to us had a puff of smoke...we have our own little nuclear bomb mushroom cloud happening. The bubbly chemicals are about to spill over the side of the beaker! No way am I going to let that toxic brew touch my fingers! The only place I can see to dump it is in the waste paper basket next to our table.

I toss the beaker like an extreme basketball shot. The beaker lands in the basket and seconds later there is an extremely loud bang, followed by even more smoke pouring from the bin. The smoke is quickly drifting across the classroom. The loud bang has finally managed to draw the attention of Mr. Facebook from his phone. He gazes in stunned horror at the room rapidly filling with smoke. Finally he screams, "Get out, FIRE!" Everyone panics and runs for the door. Mr. Facebook hits the fire alarm on his way out of the building.

The Principal looks crazed, ordering everyone to evacuate all the school buildings. Soon our class is joined on the athletics field by the whole school. I sit listening to the sound of approaching fire trucks.

Once the all-clear signal is given, Mr. Facebook marches me up to Mr. Sausage Nose's office and firmly lays the blame on me. I sit in the chair outside his office, waiting for my mom.

When Mom arrives I try to explain what happened. But Mr. Sausage Nose keeps interrupting me, saying how no other group had any problems. Mr. Facebook had told him that I wasn't listening and that is the reason why I added way too much of the chemical. When I tried to tell Mr. Sausage Nose how the teacher was on the phone instead of answering my question, he went on to praise Mr. Facebook for having the sense to use his personal phone to ring the fire and rescue. He said that if it hadn't been for his quick thinking and action…I could have burned down the whole school. "That's why he had his phone out Maddi, you must be confused," he said sternly.

"Mom, this is so unfair, it's really not my fault. I'm telling you the truth!" I shouted.

The principal started to tell Mom that I would be suspended for 4 weeks for my actions.

To my shock, my mom butted in, raising her voice, "My daughter does NOT lie! She will not be suspended, we are moving to a new school." She grabbed me by the hand and stormed out of the office.

As we drove away, Mrs. Absolutely Positive simply said,

"Maddi, don't worry, there are plenty of lovely schools to go to. There is a silver lining to every cloud of smoke."

And that's why I'm heading to my next adventure in 'My New School'.

Maddi

Story 2 - My New School

Monday

The beautiful blonde hippy woman screamed as the ninja assassin reached towards her. But just in time her slightly more beautiful and very cool 12 year-old daughter triple back flipped in between the ninja and her Mom…blocking his killer strike.

Well, not really.

In fact, the blonde hippy woman is actually my mother. My Mom is alternative with a Capital A…I hope we fit in here! And the ninja assassin is really Mr. Jones and he appears to be rather friendly for a school principal. He greeted me with a huge smile and a high five. In fact, I think that will be a much better name for my new principal, Mr. High Five.

I am the 12 year old girl who back flipped to save my

mother. Okay, I've got a very active imagination. Actually I'm not beautiful, but a bit of a plain Jane and I'm kind of almost cool, but not quite. I do like to think of myself as a child genius and funnier than a Bugs Bunny cartoon.

This is my new school, Harper Valley Elementary. I liked my old school. It was a pretty good school…before the explosion and fire. Don't get me wrong. I'm sure it will be good again, once the repairs are finished.

How was I to know that mixing a bit of this with a bit of that would cause an explosion? I bet the inventor of dynamite wasn't asked to leave his school!

Mom and Dad split a couple of months before my invention incident. After the incident, it was suggested that my Mom should find a school more suitable. This wasn't a very good start to the year!

My Mom, I call her Mrs. Absolutely Positive, says this is just another small step on the journey of life and as one door closes…another will open.

Going to a new school, where I don't know anyone, where I don't know where anything is or any of the teachers, is "a great opportunity" for me, according to my Mom.

Now you know why I call her Mrs. Absolutely Positive. She thinks that hanging a crystal around my neck will protect me and solve all my problems. The only way that crystal is going to help me, is if I swallow it and have to be medevac'd out of here.

Mr. High Five has been "going on" for about 20 minutes now and has introduced his Deputy. No high fives or even a smile from her. Just a not so brief summary of the 5000 and 1 rules of Harper Valley School, complete with the details of punishments. I think I'll call her Mrs. She Who Runs The

School.

Oh goody, we have finally finished the enrolment, now I get to go to my new class and meet the teacher…and be stared at and evaluated by thirty other kids.

7A is my new class, the A is for amazing, says my new teacher. She prattled on for a good ten minutes about how much I will enjoy my new class, how lovely the children are, how learning is fun and we'll be doing so much learning that it will be fun every second of every day.

Yeah sure. Five hours cooped up in a small room with 30 other children, all with various body odor problems with activities ranging from mind melting boredom to fun extension work. You know, the kind of work that makes you feel like a mental midget. I think I'll call her, Miss Learning Is Fun.

After careful consideration on how to further destroy my life, Miss Learning Is Fun chooses a lovely seat for me next to what appears to be a living fossil, "The Cave Man". Burt is about 10 foot tall, 10 foot wide and has more hair on his knuckles than I have on my head. He raises his eyebrows and grunts what I think is hello, as I take my seat.

Just like Mom said, "A fresh new start will be marvelous for you."

As I sit in the shadow of Burt, I scan the class for signs of intelligent life forms. I see the usual standard mix for any class. The popular girls, the footy boys (that explains some of the odors), the nerds and scattered around are the weirdoes.

A few kids seem almost normal and could be worthy of further investigation. Especially a tall, dark and handsome boy…who actually appears to be able to read.

As I sit eating dinner that night, my organic tofu and enough salad to feed an army of bunnies, Mom gushes, "I bet you had a great day".

"How many new friends did you make?" I mumble "none", but she seems not to hear, but continues on about how I should make it a goal to make a new friend every day, so by the end of the year…the whole school will be my friend.

Yeah right, then perhaps I could move on to the billions in China. After our compulsory ritual of 30 minutes of yoga and meditation, Mom sends me off to bed with a "remember the early bird gets the worm" talk. I wonder what the girls with normal mothers are doing? Eating a cheeseburger while watching TV probably, oh those poor poor children.

Tuesday

I HATE swimming!

Oh I can swim okay. I can even put on my swim cap and adjust my goggles so they don't become mini swimming pools for my eyes. Some kids swim like dolphins, sleek and smooth through the water. However I swim more like a hippo, just my eyes showing above the surface and a LOT of kicking and splashing! I can make the 50, but if you come to watch you might just want a snack to tide you over as you wait for me to finish.

After my school swimming lesson today, I HATE SWIMMING even more!

It all started going wrong when Mum presented me with a new swimsuit. It was the height of fashion, about 100 years ago! You know the type, a lovely floral number with some frills in all the wrong places. I know that sounds horrible, but I hid my feelings from my Mom. She always tries her best. So I smiled and thanked her. I even kept smiling when she gave me a matching swim cap.

Mrs. Absolutely Positive then assured me that they are a one off outfit, totally unique and will help me to stand out from the crowd. Thanks Mom, that's just what every 12 year old girl wants to do, stand out and be totally different.

I know that all this sounds really sarcastic, but with you Dear Diary, I can say what I think. I am an expert at the blank look. Nobody can read my thoughts. But I have to tell someone. I have to get it all out.

Now my Mom may be alternative (hippy clothes, a piercing on her nose and a tattoo on her ankle) but she is very efficient. She has carefully and clearly labeled all my clothes and belongings with my name. It seemed a really good idea at the time…before today that is.

Swimming was our second lesson of the day and we hurried out to the bus after English.

The trip on the bus is loud, smelly and hot. Do kids who are 12 really sing 'The Wheels On The Bus'? Yes, they do at Harper Valley and Miss Learning Is Fun cheerfully led them through each verse. Really, have they not heard of the radio or a CD?

We finally arrive and have to share the change room with a class of little kids. This is when my first mistake of the day happens. You know how your Mom always says to wear good undies when you go out? Well, I didn't. My undies had a couple of holes, but worst of all they had Dora The Explorer on them. (Mum thought they looked adorable when she bought them, she thought the picture was a hoola girl, not a little kid's character.)

Anyway, as I changed into my unique and attention grabbing swim suit, I became aware of the joy and amusement I was causing. Little girls and my classmates were all staring and laughing at my swimmers, some even pointed in case I was in any doubt that I was the focus of their attention.

So I hurriedly stuffed all my clothes into my bag, or so I thought and ran outside waiting at the edge of the pool. My class on one side and the little kids on the other side.

Then I saw the pool attendant walking out of the change rooms, a pair of undies extended into the air on the end of her fingertips. I recognized them immediately. Then the whole scene went into agonizing slow motion.

She goes across to the little kids and holds the undies up. Nobody claims them, so she heads over to our class. She does a great job of holding them up. Dora is clearly identifiable and the holes clearly visible. Her fingers are covering up the name tag, so she can't see my name. Thank goodness! Nobody is going to know that the ultimate in embarrassing undies is mine, what a relief. The attendant walks away, now I can breathe again and focus on surviving swimming.

'Screeeeech'! The pool's loudspeaker system squawks to life. "Attention please, attention please, I have a lost pair of girl's underwear, they have a lovely picture of Dora The Explorer on both the front and back…hang on, there is a name tag, Maddi Bull, Maddi Bull, please come to the counter to collect your underwear."

I try to disappear into the cracks in the concrete, but to no avail. Miss Learning Is Fun calls from the front of the line, "That's why it is so important to name everything, quick Maddi, go and collect your undies straight away."

The walk of shame begins. Past my class (most were sniggering), past the little kids (even they were smirking) and past the wrinklies who were doing their slow motion water aerobics. One of the little kids called out, "Cool undies!" Another yelled, "I love Dora too!" Great, I'm a legend with 5 year olds!

I return to my class and prepare to face my next ordeal, the swim. Many laps later, I cuddle the lane rope and try to get my breath back. The little kids are in the pool now, at least I can swim better than them (well, most of them).

The swim coach calls us out of the pool. Now he wants us to dive in and retrieve plastic rings. Fantastic, I'm good at diving! I breeze through this. Then he makes it into a contest. Two kids at time, the winner moves on and the loser is eliminated. Round after round I win, this is my big chance to impress my classmates. I can gain respect, be cool and make up for the undies incident.

It is down to me and the leader of the cool girls' group. Her name is Mandy the Mermaid (not her real name). The coach tosses the ring in and blows his whistle. We hit the water together. I kick as hard as I can and reach down. I grab it and raise my hand in triumph. Except when I look at Mandy the Mermaid she is holding the ring in her hand. The faces of the class and coach have a strange look of horror pasted on them.

One of the little kids has had an accident. It isn't the plastic ring I am holding. I'm holding a ring of poo! I scream and toss it away. The looks of horror turn into howls of laughter. I feel like diving to the bottom to escape, but what is lurking underwater is even worse than facing my class.

"No Mom, I didn't have fun at swimming. Can we move to the desert?"

Friday

Cooking today, no worries, I can cook toast, 2 minute noodles and virtually anything you can reheat in a microwave oven.

I like the cooking class already. My teacher's name is Mrs. Muffin, real name is Mrs. Moffat. As she was going through the kitchen rules, I was warping her body into a muffin and dusting her with icing sugar.

Actually she is great. She made us all put on hair nets. You should have heard the groans and whinging from the cool girls. Covering up their shiny gorgeous hair makes them look normal. Yaayyy!

Remember I told you about a tall, dark and handsome boy who caught my attention on my first day? Well obviously his name is: Mr. Tall Dark and Handsome. Well, Mrs. Muffin paired me up with – Mr. Tall Dark and Handsome himself!!!! And a funny geeky looking girl called Gretel.

Things are starting to turn around. This might be my chance to impress. I look at the recipe and ingredients, oops, no mention of reheating in the microwave. We have to make chicken in apricot sauce and vegetables. A bit more complicated than I had hoped for, but never fear, Gretel appears to know what she is doing. I think she is some kind of master chef. Already she is dicing and slicing, leaving me plenty of time to talk to Mr. Tall, Dark and Handsome.

Soon Gretel has everything ready to go into the oven. I think I might let Gretel work with me every cooking lesson, she's fantastic! As she pops the food into the oven, Mrs. Muffin tells her that her brother is sick and she has to go home early. I have to stop interrogating (I mean talking to) Mr. Tall Dark and Handsome and take over.

It was then that I realized we were alone and I had no idea what to do next. Not the slightest idea of how long to cook the chicken dish for. I don't want to be totally uncool and let him know I am useless at cooking, so I just have to work it out. Let's see, noodles take 2 minutes max, and the microwave meals mum cooks take 10 minutes. The school ovens are big and fan forced, so they'll probably cook heaps faster. So I'm guessing 5 minutes should do it. But just to be safe, I'll leave it in for 6 minutes.

What a star! I pull the dish out right on 6 minutes and we are the first group to finish. Mrs. Muffin is really impressed. None of the other groups are anywhere near finished. Is that the smell of an A for cooking???

She decides to do a taste test and scoops a big spoonful into her mouth. All the kids gather round in awe. As she chews, her face contorts and she seems to gasp for air. Suddenly she vomits my apricot chicken all over Mr. Tall Dark and handsome and several nearby students.

"That chicken is RAW!!!" she screams. So cooking class ends early, looks like an E on my report for cooking. Mr. Tall Dark and Handsome stares at me in disbelief and walks away. And Mrs. Muffin now has a new name, Mrs. Chew and Spew.

Thank goodness I have the weekend to get over my cooking failure.

Monday

After a short interview with Mr. High Five and She Who Rules the School I am cleared of deliberately trying to poison the cooking teacher and am merely found guilty of gross stupidity. The principal gives me a high 5 as I leave. And the deputy quietly snarls at me, "I'm keeping an eye on you."

I hurry off to my English class, but by the time I get there it has already started. The teacher looks grumpy already. I like to call him Mr. Albert because his frizzy wild hair looks like it was done by Albert Einstein's hairdresser.

"Madonna, we've just finished reading everyone's essays on 'The Merchant of Venice', pass me yours and I'll read it because we really need to get on with today's work."

I fumble in my bag for my English book, but accidently pull out my diary instead. It is covered in the same dark pink paper that Mom covered all my books in. Mr. Albert starts to read in his loud, clear voice. Oh no! I made this diary entry last night, when I was multi-tasking my English homework and diary dreaming.

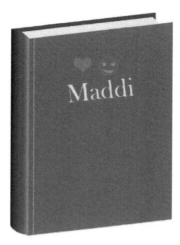

The quality of mercy is not strained…but falls like the gentle rain. Mercy, I wish that Mr. Albert would give me some mercy and sit me next to that hunky Richard Jones. I just love his curly hair and those hazel eyes. Mr. Albert comes to a stop and there is a moment of complete silence before the whole class bursts into spasms of laughter and cheering.

The only people not laughing are Richard Jones and me. We appear to be having a blushing competition with no clear winner.

Oh, the teacher isn't laughing either. He asks me who Mr. Albert is. I tell him it is just my imagination. The bell rings and I try to disappear to the darkest corner of the library. I've decided to research if NASA needs any 12 year old girls to send into space, TODAY!!!

Lunch…the loneliest word for losers like me. The student body seems to be divided into two groups. Those who think I am a complete idiot and just laugh at me. And those who think I am a crazy fool and just want to stay away from me. I sit in the far eating corner, alone with my bean and tofu salad. It always seems that my life is destined to appear on the TV show World's Worst Disasters.

As I sit with my head down, a shadow falls across me. I don't dare look up, it is probably someone who has come to tease me about one of my stupid antics.

"Hi, that looks like a nice salad." I look up and see Gretel smiling down at me. She sits besides me and tells me how she feels sorry for me about the cooking incident and the diary mistake. She continues on about how we should work together in the next cooking class because she can help me. I look at her in shock, is she insane!!!!

Lunch time passes quickly as we talk about our families and

the friends we wish we had.

Hey Mom, I think I may have made a new friend.

Wednesday

New Day...New Lesson.

I sit confidently beside Gretel in Science. My history with science is not good and that's why I'm letting Gretel take the lead role.

Our science teacher looks like a scientist with thick red hair. She also teaches me math (well, she can try!) I think I'll call her Mrs. Red.

Anyway, all is going well...Gretel and I have gathered the test tubes, beakers, bunsen burner, matches, safety goggles and an assortment of materials. Quickly we use our superior skills to read through the procedure and set up our equipment.

Mrs. Red has positioned herself in front of our bench. She's keeping an eye on the pair of jocks that appear to be having trouble. What a pity she has her back to us and can't see what a great job we are doing.

Gretel skillfully mixes the substances in the beaker of tap water, while I time how long it takes to dissolve. Next we heat the bunsen burner to see how long it takes to dissolve in hot water.

I play it safe and leave the lighting of the bunsen burner to Gretel. Perhaps I shouldn't have told her about my experiences at my last school. Four matches later and still no flame. I urged Gretel to put the match closer. But she put it too close and actually jams the match into the gas nozzle, where it gets stuck!

That's when I have a brain wave. I'll turn the gas up full blast and that will probably blow the match out of the nozzle. I probably should have told Gretel about my plan. Just as the gas handle reaches maximum flow, Gretel lights another match. The stuck match shoots out and hits the flame on Gretel's match with a huge whoosh!!!!!

So there you have it. Our bunsen burner is now a flame-thrower that any Xbox gamer would be proud of. We watch in horror as the flame races towards Mrs. Red's head. The flame just reaches the ends of her wild hair. I turn the gas off and Gretel throws the beaker of water at her hair.

Mrs. Red turns around and yells, "What are you girls doing!!!!"

Gretel apologizes, "Sorry Miss, I tripped and spilled the water." She really didn't know what had just happened. She didn't know that her hair had been on fire. "Well hurry up girls, you haven't even got your bunsen burner turned on yet," she snaps.

I mouth a "thank you" to Gretel and she just smiles and says, "That's what friends are for."

The rest of the day passed without incident. After the close shave in science, I kind of like boring.

Monday

PE lesson time with Mr. Arnie. Now Mr. Arnie is BIG and I mean BIG in a fit muscular way. I feel that Mr. Arnie is a much better name than Mr. Jones (his real name) as he really does look like the school's own Terminator.

He walks us over to the climbing wall. I think he plans to terminate me! Great an activity that combines my fear of heights and my natural lack of coordination, what can possibly go wrong? I hope the school nurse isn't busy.

Mr. Arnie puts us into teams and guess what!!! Mr. Tall Dark and Handsome is my partner! I tell him that my climbing experience is limited to climbing out of bed in the morning. So he volunteers to go first. What a gentleman! He really is quite nice. Today is my chance to make an impression and really connect with him. Mr. Tall Dark and Handsome puts on his safety harness and gets ready to climb. And I am his safety person, I have to hang onto the safety rope to make sure he doesn't slip off the hand holds and fall to the ground.

Well Mr. Tall Dark and Handsome isn't exactly Spiderman, but he moves quite well and rapidly approaches the top. Soon he'll be back on his way down and my fringe is hanging in my eyes. I try to move my hair, it really needs a flick back. The trouble is that both my hands are on the safety rope. He's climbing well and looking very secure. I'll just hold the rope with one hand and fix my hair.

The cry from above and jerk on the rope happen at the same time. The rope whirls through my hand before I can get both hands back on. Mr. Tall Dark and Handsome only falls about a body length, but he manages to bounce his head against the wall quite hard.

Mr. Arnie rushes over and helps lower him to the ground. Mr. Tall Dark and Handsome (Mr. TDH) is really quite good about it. He says the swelling black eye doesn't hurt that much. He tells me that it could happen to anyone.

Then he helps me put on my harness and gives me advice on which handholds to use first. He is sooooo nice!!!! I really want to impress him and set out determined to reach the top. I'm going really well. This isn't going to be as hard as I thought. I risk a quick look down at him. BIG MISTAKE!!! I seem so high, my heart begins to pound and my hands start to sweat. I can't move my legs. I'm frozen to the spot.

I'm like one of those little lizards that grip to a wall, motionless, so predators can't see them. Except my strength is running out. My arms and legs begin to shake. Mr. TDH yells encouragement, so does Mr. Arnie. I glance down again and realize I'm the last one on the wall and the rest of the class has finished and are gazing up at me. I must go on, I use all my willpower and reach up with my right hand to the hold. My fingers brush it, but slip off. I stretch further and push with my legs using all my remaining strength. My sweat soaked fingers on my right hand slip off the hand hold. Time seems to stand still for a few seconds, I can hear my heart thumping.

Then I try to reach the hold again but my frantic efforts cause my upper body to swing out from the wall. In a flash I'm hanging upside down! Thank goodness Mr. TDH is better on the safety ropes than me.

I look down to see where I am, but I can't see anything. My loose gym shirt has fallen over my face. The crowd below can't see my blushing face but they can see my sports bra! And I stayed upside down for 2 minutes while they lowered me down to the ground.

The gasps of shock as I first fell have quickly turned to laughter. If laughter is truly the best medicine, then my classmates are going to be very healthy. I wanted to make an impression on Mr. TDH, but not this way!

When I finally reach the ground, Mr. TDH turns away while I readjust my top and then assures me that I'm okay with a concerned look in his eyes.

Maybe today wasn't a COMPLETE disaster after all.

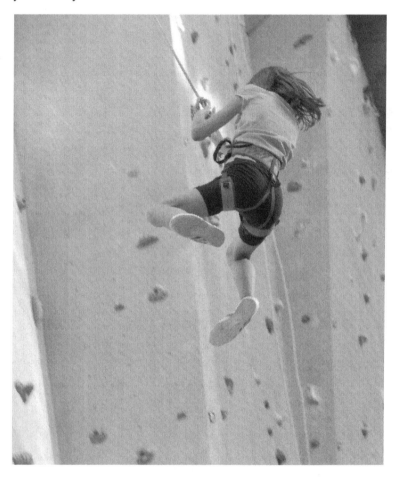

Friday

"Wake up darling, I've got a surprise for you!" calls my mom (with her way too happy for 7am in the morning voice). A surprise! The last surprise Mom got for me was a week long Buddhist enlightment course, where they shaved my head, fed me grains, nuts and vegetables and had me either chanting or sitting in silence all day long. I had to wear a hat for 6 months until my hair grew back!

Reluctantly I head downstairs to find Mom smiling and holding up a costume. "Try it on," she says. Now I don't know about you, but I never win an argument with my mom, so I figured I can spend 15 minutes asking why, saying I'm too old to dress up in costumes and that I don't want to try it on or I can just do it now. So I put it on. The red, white and blue Supergirl costume is actually pretty nice. I love the shiny red boots and the blue cape. Actually the shorts and top look pretty good on me. And the eye mask really sets off the costume.

As I stand there looking like an aspiring student from Super Hero College, Mom pulls out the camera and starts clicking away.

I check myself in the mirror. Super Hero red and blue just might be my colors. And in a strange way, the eye mask does seem to accentuate my eyes. As I stand there admiring myself, I suddenly think...why has Mom got me this costume?

When I ask her, she explains that she saw in the school's newsletter that today is dress up day. I didn't know that. I ask Mom if she is sure and she is absolutely certain! I go looking for the newsletter, but in her efficient and environmentally friendly way, she has put it in the recycling bin, which was collected yesterday.

Oh well, I do look good and I'm sure Mr. TDH will think so too.

Mom even offers to drop me off at the school gate so I don't crush my cape on the school bus. I'll get there early giving more people the chance to see how fantastic I look.

I strut into the school grounds with my cape billowing in the breeze. The first few kids I see don't have costumes on, they just stare at me. Really some people never join in on days like this. I wait near my classroom and watch as more and more kids arrive. Problem, so far nobody else has a costume on! By the time the bell goes I'm hiding in the toilets. And I still haven't seen any other costumes.

I wait for a few more minutes to let the hall clear and then rush into my classroom. As I burst through the door, someone has left their bag lying just inside the doorway. I trip over it and fly through the air in my best Supergirl pose. The class burst into laughter (they are getting healthy again) while mercifully my cape falls over my face. The laughter dies down. Miss Learning Is Fun starts clapping and smiles at me. "Wow Madonna, what a creative entry into the room, but dress up day isn't until next week dear."

At home that afternoon Mom says, "I bet you had a great day, did everyone like your costume?" "Yes Mom, I really did stand out...thanks to you." She smiled at me with such a look of love, "No need to thank me dear, that's what moms are for."

Friday

Two weeks have passed and I've had NO dramas! And no, I didn't dress up the following week. It is so nice to be normal. Mr. TDH has talked to me a few times, he's really nice!

Monday

On my way to lunch today I saw 2 lines at the student center. I wonder what I didn't hear about this time. I notice Gretel, three from the front of one of the lines. Ignoring the dirty looks I slink down next to her and ask why she is lining up. She tells me you have to put your name down if you want to have a School Fair and you're happy to help out on the day. She tells me how great it will be, "We'll have carnival rides and junk food galore, you've got to put your name down!" "Just line up with me." The girl behind Gretel hisses at me and gives me a filthy look. So I go to the back of the line, behind about 30 kids.

After a few minutes, Gretel gives me a wave as she walks off. This is going to take FOREVER!!!! I look at the other line, it is much shorter, so I swap over. Honestly, some people have no brains! The line I left is still so long and the one I swapped to is almost empty. I quickly put my name down and go and sit with Gretel to have lunch.

After lunch, when I'm happily daydreaming in English, Mr. Vale, the arts teacher, enters our classroom. Mr. Vale is tall and slightly stooped. His head is balding. He has a big fat nose that is out of proportion with the rest of his face. The way he moves with his head thrust slightly forward and his black beady eyes kind of reminds me of a bald eagle. So naturally I call him Mr. Eagle. Now Mr. Eagle is VERY intense and to be honest a little scary. Most arts teachers are all light and happy, dancing and singing their way around the school. But not Mr. Eagle! He moans and groans a LOT and only seems happy when he is failing some poor kid for their lack of artistic skills.

Mr. Eagle holds a list of names and announces the following people are to report to the hall before school tomorrow for auditions in the school musical, Swan Lake. So you can imagine my horror when he called out my name. A mistake! A horrible mistake!! I can't sing!!! And I can't dance!!!! Me in a musical, no way!

I raise my hand. The beady eyes swivel to me and I nervously tell Mr. Eagle that there has been a mistake, I didn't sign up for the musical. He struts over to me. His hot and coffee smelling breath in my face, "Is this your handwriting?" he snarls. I've stopped breathing, it is my signature. My head drops and I nod my head yes.

Mr. Eagle then launches into a speech about commitment and following through with promises. Then it hits me, 2 lines! I didn't put my name down for the school fair, I put it down for the musical.

I told Mom when I got home. I hoped she might ring him. But no, she thinks I'll be brilliant in a musical. She went on and on about how she wished she would have had this wonderful opportunity when she went to school…

Tuesday

I got to the hall on time. All the talented kids were waiting outside. I felt so out of place! Mr. Eagle sits on a chair in front of the stage and calls us in one at a time. We had to go on stage and sing a song from a song book on a stand. I'm about mid-group and I feel like throwing up. The girls before me are warming their voices up. They sound like they should be competing on American Idol.

Finally my turn arrives. I trip on the stairs on the way up to the stage and knock the stand over. A glance at Mr. Eagle shows those beady black eyes staring at me. No smile, no encouragement.

My voice changes pitch as I struggle through the first few lines of the song. "Enough," he shouts. I ask if I can go now and he gives me a second helping of his commitment speech and tells me to wait to the left, so I can try out for a dancing part.

As I wait for the singing auditions to end, I check out the dancing girls. They all have two things in common, dancing shoes and leotards. I get the feeling that I am the only person here whose dancing experience only consists of dancing in front of the TV to the Wiggles.

Eventually Mr. Eagle calls us onto the stage. He wants us all to dance together, at the same time. Phew!!!! What a relief! I can hide at the back. He quickly shows us a "simple" routine that we have to perform. The music starts and everyone takes 4 quick steps to the left, except me, unfortunately I go to the right. Then we had to move forward 4 steps and twirl. I collide with the two girls in front of me and send them sprawling to the floor. "Enough!" roars Mr. Eagle. "Will I go now?" I meekly ask him. I get the commitment speech again and he tells me to wait off stage.

P.s. Two months later, after many rehearsals we finally put on Swan Lake. Mum picks me up at the back of the hall after I've removed my make up and changed out of my costume. "Oh Madonna, I was so proud of you. You were such a great tree," Mom gushes.

Wednesday

I stand gazing at the noticeboard.

Keep Our School Clean POSTER Competition, reads the notice. A one day free pass for three people for Waterslide World is the prize for the winning entry.

As I stand there dreaming, Gretel rocks up. "We should have a go at making a poster," she prompts me. Then Mr. TDH arrives with his smile and asks if he can work with us on making a poster. Going to Waterslide World with my two friends, now that would be very cool!

Later as we sit around and brainstorm ideas, we discover Mr. TDH is a computer wiz. He is highly skilled with computer graphics and editing pictures. Just what you need to create a winning entry.

With a shy smile, Mr. TDH suggests we need a superhero to clean up rubbish on our poster and asks if he can get a few photos of me in my costume because I look so good in it.

WOW!!!!! Of course I agree!

Thursday

After school I change into my costume and we get some shots.

Meanwhile, I come up with this little rhyme to go with the poster (inspired by Mom's favorite singer – John Lennon).

IMAGINE THERE IS NO RUBBISH...ANYWHERE IN THE WORLD...NO CHOKING TURTLES...NO PAPER ON THE GROUND...IMAGINE ALL THE PEOPLE...PICKING UP ALL THEIR JUNK...WHAT A CLEAN PLACE IT WOULD BE...SO CLEAN FOR YOU AND ME.

BTW Mom loves this! I think it is a bit corny, but I can't think of anything else.

In no time at all, with Mr. TDH's skills we have a great poster entered into the competition. And we are getting closer!

Monday

At last we reach the day they announce the winners of the poster competition. All the students are gathered in the hall, waiting expectantly. Mr. High Five, high fives his way to the center stage with a sheet of paper in his hand. I close my eyes and hope. Mr. High Five announces we have many great entries, but only one can win. "And the winner is....." I open my eyes to see our poster on the data projector screen. Gretel's screaming drowns the rest of his words. But it doesn't matter, we have WON!!!!

Gretel, Mr. TDH and I go up to the stage where Mr. High Five shakes our hands and presents us with the free pass. I can't believe it! I'm on stage and everyone in the hall is clapping and cheering for me. And I'm standing next to my two best friends.

You know, I think I'm going to love my time at Harper Valley School.

Sunday

The day finally arrives. Yes, Gretel, Mr. Tall Dark and Handsome and I take on Waterslide World. I am both excited and nervous. The three of us have free passes for Waterslide World.

According to the website it has: *The biggest and best waterslides in the world featuring the longest black hole, fully enclosed waterslide ever built.*

I was so excited about winning - but now the day is here I am a bit worried. You see, I have always had a bit of fear about heights and enclosed spaces. So the biggest waterslides equals **high waterslides with big drops**. And fully enclosed black hole slide equals **dark enclosed space** equals **FEAR FACTOR OF 10!!!!!**

Mom drops us off at Waterslide World just as it opens. The attendant collects our passes and issues us with waterproof armbands complete with a barcode that gives us access to a locker to put our money and dry clothes in. We quickly put our valuables and dry clothes in the locker and just keep our towels with us.

Mom lathered us up with sunscreen before we came and we

all are wearing Lycra wet shirts so we don't have to worry about getting sun burnt.

Most of the slides end in the same pool. It is enormous and has a marked off area where you can just swim if you want and a shallow section for little kids. Around the edge of the pool are a heap of deck chairs, we figure we might want to have a rest later, so we leave our towels spread out on three of the deck chairs.

Then we check out the park map and head for our first slide. It is a slide called The Terror Tower. It is an open slide and despite its name doesn't seem that high. We walk up the steps and this takes a lot longer than I expected. Finally, we reach the top and Mr. TDH starts raving about the view. He keeps pointing out the landmarks we can see… I nod and smile but stop looking after the first one. This ride is a lot taller than I thought.

We wait for our turn, Mr. TDH is rapidly turning into Mr. Talkative, while Gretel is strangely quiet. As I look at Gretel I notice that she is also very pale. When I asked her if she is okay, she gushes out how she has never been to any amusement park and is feeling really scared. As I try to calm her and tell her how I'm scared too, Mr. TDH listens intently. "Thank goodness," he finally says, "I thought I was the only one who was scared."

Suddenly it's our turn and the attendant hands us a foam mat to sit on to go down the slide. Mr. TDH bravely volunteers to go down first and rapidly disappears from sight. Gretel goes next… And I can tell when she reaches the bottom because that's when her screaming stops. Then it's my turn. I go swooshing down the slide…as fast as a rocket. My ride is over before I know it and I splash into the pool at the end. "That was great!" I yell to Gretel and Mr. TDH who are waiting for me in the pool. (Mr. TDH really has the nicest smile.)

Perhaps I'm not such a chicken after all. Mr. TDH and Gretel seem to have overcome their fears and together we run up the stairs to the second of many more slides on the Terror Tower. We try three other similar open slides and conquer all of them. Even though Gretel is having a ball, she still screams for the whole length of every slide. I didn't realize that girl had such a great set of lungs.

Next we head for an even bigger slide, which runs straight down with a couple of bumps along the way. It's called the River Of Doom. Really, where do they get these names from, don't they know some little children could be scared! On this slide you sit on a little rubber boat, one person on each side facing backwards and one lucky person gets to sit at the very back to face forwards. On the walk up to the top, I notice that the back seat is the way to go, without fail those people facing backwards going down the slide - scream all the way down to the bottom.

I try to distract Gretel and Mr. TDH from watching the boats going down the slide. I pointed out the great view of the other slides, how well-made the steps are and how close the sun is. However, I don't think my distractions have worked because when the attendant calls us forward for our go, both Gretel and Mr. TDH take off like rockets trying to get to the backseat first. The floor of the boat is wet and slippery and as Gretel and Mr. TDH each try to maneuver into the seat, I do the only sensible thing possible...I give them a huge shove sending them both sprawling into the boat, while I slide into the back seat. They pick themselves up and glare at me as they sit in the backward facing seats.

"You know guys, this ride doesn't look half as scary when you can see where you are going," I chirp happily. Perhaps I shouldn't rub it in, but I did outsmart both of them and I can't help myself.

The attendant gives me a peculiar smile as he starts to push the boat towards the edge. I guess he was impressed by how I outmaneuvered my friends to get the best seat. Just as our boat is about to go over the edge, he looks at me and says, "Enjoy your ride." Then he spins the boat around so that Gretel and Mr. TDH are facing forwards and now I am facing backwards. ARRRHHHHH!!!!! I scream all the way down. I sound as bad as Gretel. After that, I have to buy both Gretel and Mr. TDH an ice cream before they forgive me.

We decide to have a break… walking up all those stairs to the slides is pretty exhausting. So we head to our towels and deck chairs. Gretel and Mr. TDH grab their towels and start to dry off. But I have a problem. I feel like Goldilocks - someone has been sleeping on my deck chair. Someone is laying on my towel! And still is! A very large man, looking a bit like that famous wrestler - Hulk Hogan...and he is sound asleep on my deck chair.

Now I don't care about the deck chair, but I do care about my towel. It is a lovely blue and yellow one that Mom gave to me for my birthday last year. Mr. Giant is asleep so deeply, that he is snoring really loudly, as loud as a jumbo jet taking off. About every fourth snore, he lets off a shuddering snort. Gross!!!!! A waterslide park is not a quiet place, so I don't know how he can sleep through all the noise, but his sleeping is about to stop. I go to tap him on the shoulder, when Mr. TDH grabs my arm and whispers, "Don't." Why is he whispering, I don't know, it would appear no noise could wake the sleeping giant. Mr. TDH tells me that he once read that waking the person in a deep sleep can be dangerous, as they could get a fright and lash out. Well I don't want Mr. Giant lashing out, he could flatten all three of us accidentally.

Then I have a light bulb moment, I come up with a brilliant idea. A corner of my towel is hanging out over the edge of the deck chair, maybe I can pull it out from underneath him. I give it a tug, nothing happens, I tug as hard as I can, but still no towel. I call Gretel and Mr. TDH over and we all pull together with a mighty heave. The towel doesn't barge nor does the giant, but we end up falling into a heap on top of each other.

Then Mr. TDH comes up with an even better idea and dashes off to buy a can of soft drink. Did I mention that it is a really hot day and if you fell asleep laying in the sun - you would be feeling really, really hot! Anyway, we take turns in shaking up the can. Then we climb into the pool (luckily the giant is on a deck chair that is quite close to the edge of the pool). Mr. TDH takes careful aim with the can and pops the lid. The last thing we see before we duck beneath the water is almost the entire contents of the can (as a frothy icy shower) spurting towards Mr. Giant's back.

We hold our breath for as long as we can and when we pop up Mr. Giant is standing up and wiping the soft drink off with my towel. He chucks the towel on the deck chair and storms off towards the park office with a fierce scowl on his face. We leap from the pool, grab our towels and head for the opposite end of the park.

MISSION ACCOMPLISHED!!!! (In your head play the Mission Impossible sound track.)

What a day, we have had so much fun - but before we go home we have decided to tackle our fears and ride the black hole waterslide. Two minutes and 42 seconds of falling in total darkness! Yes, we are nuts!!!!!

We make the ascent to the top of the black hole with shaking legs and nervous bellies. We stand and watch the other people taking off for a while, trying to build up our courage. I noticed some kids using two mats and I ask one teenage girl why. She tells me that it makes you go faster.

While I ponder this new information, Gretel starts grabbing at my arm and pointing at the steps. It's Mr. Eagle, the music teacher. I'd recognize that glistening bald head and weird walk anywhere. Mr. Eagle isn't our favorite teacher and everyone finds those beady eyes that stare through you so intimidating.

Suddenly the pressure is on. We all want to go down the slide before Mr. Eagle arrives. Finally we reach the front of the line and Mr. TDH grabs a mat from the pile and launches himself down the tube. Gretel is next. With her face set in grimace, she half falls and half jumps into the tube. As per usual, I can hear Gretel screaming all the way down. (Now that really doesn't help with my confidence!)

I'm just not ready to go yet. The thought of being in the black tube is just overwhelming! I step aside and let two other people go. The attendant is a young teenage boy and he is spending more time on his phone than supervising the slide. "Excuse me," I say "can I grab an extra mat?" He mumbles sure without even looking at me. I look around and see that Mr. Eagle is going to end up standing in line behind me. That's it! I'm out of here! I want to go now and fast.

That's when I get a brilliant idea. I was going to grab two mats because that other kid said it makes you go faster. So if I grab more than two mats, I should go even faster. The attendant isn't looking, so I start grabbing the mats and stacking them on top of each other. I start with one for my body and one for my legs, then add two more layers on top. Six mats - I'm going to fly down that tube. I sneak a quick glance back at Mr. Eagle, I don't think he has recognized me with my face plastered in sunscreen and my hair looking like a wet mop.

I get on the mats and try to push off, but nothing happens. I hear Mr. Eagles voice behind me, "Hey kid, you've got too many mats!" Suddenly my mats start to move in the water flow going into the black hole and I'm off! As I hit the first bend in the darkness – I scream! This is so fast and scary. I hit a really sharp bend and I feel the mats shift under me. The next thing I know, I am tumbling along upside down leaving a trail of mats behind me. Eventually I stop and in the dark I grope around and my fingers touch a mat. I pull it closer and sit on it. Hang on - why aren't I moving? It's the water flow, it has slowed down to a tiny trickle - hardly enough to provide enough lubrication for the mat to slide. I give a few pushes with my hands and slowly I start to move again. Eventually I reach the end, but instead of chickening out the end...I kind of stopped at the edge and have to jump out. Gretel and Mr. TDH are waiting in the pool and stare at me in bewilderment.

Then we hear the pool attendant on his walkie-talkie, "Tell the black hole attendant to stop the ride and don't let anyone else go down the slide as there must be a blockage." Mr. TDH asks, "How could the slides get blocked?" Before the attendant can answer, we all hear a faint boom, boom sound and muffled yelling. We all look around wondering where it is coming from. Suddenly the attendant gasps, "Someone is trapped in the slide!"

He races off and within minutes workers are tapping along the outside of the slide trying to find where the trapped person is. A worker has found the blockage mid-slide. Quickly they undo the massive bolts that hold the slide together. As most of the park visitors stand around watching, they lift the top half of the section off. Revealing a stack of five mats blocking the slide and squashed up against the mats is a very angry looking Mr. Eagle. "It was that silly girl in front of me," he splutters, "I told her she had too many mats."

I grab Mr. TDH and Gretel by their arms and quickly lead them over to grab our gear and head for the exit. We have had a great day, but it is definitely time to leave!

He's Back!

I sense the presence in my room before I hear anything. I hold my breath and try to still my racing heart as I strain my ears to hear any sound. I hear the floorboards creak, that's probably what woke me in the first place. I hear loud breathing, almost panting and a scratching sound on the polished wooden floorboards of my bedroom. Slowly I gather my nerve and start to turn around in my bed to face it. My bed creaks and I cringe and stop. The breathing seems to be closer now so I quickly turn all the way over.

Before me stands a tall, black fur covered creature with a mouthful of glistening white fangs. It's Tyson, my Dad's Great Dane dog. That can only mean one thing, Dad's back.

As I try to get out of bed, Tyson greets me with a low "woof" and happily wags his giant tail. In two quick wags his tail sweeps all of my stuff from my dressing table. Tyson then leans against me as Great Danes tend to do and knocks me back into bed. He comes over and gives me a big sloppy lick before he trots out of my bedroom. I follow Tyson out to the lounge room to find Mom and Dad deep in conversation.

Mom and Dad split up about six months ago. I still spoke to Dad every week on the phone. Mom, in her hippy alternative way, said Dad needed to rediscover himself and it was just part of his life journey. I think he was just having a mid-life crisis (as did Mom) but I was still shocked to see him at our new home.

My Dad is a big tall man with brown hair. It is short now, it used to be long and he had a ponytail. I think he looks better with short hair, more "normal". He also has a big booming voice. Seriously he could stun a cat at fifty yards and rattle windows at a hundred yards. That's why I often refer to him as Mr. Boom Boom. Think sonic boom but with a human sound.

Mom then announced the great news, Dad is coming back to live with us. I feel so happy, I love my Dad so much and having my parents back together is so fantastic!

Sunday

Aloha! Hawaii Here We Come!

Dad has a great idea, we are going on a holiday to Hawaii. A chance to reconnect and reharvest our energies so our family can achieve harmony again, so now you can see why Dad is married to my hippy alternative Mom or as I call her Mrs. Absolutely-Positive. Actually, he really shouldn't have had the ponytail cut off, my parents are like hippies. But that is cool for me (most of the time) because they are so loving and open.

I've never been on a plane, and to be honest I feel a bit scared. I don't understand how something that big and heavy can fly in the air. When I asked, couldn't we just drive to Hawaii, Mom and Dad just laughed. After Dad explained that I would have my own DVD player to watch during the flight and that the cabin crew would bring me food and drinks, I decided it couldn't be that bad.

The take off was loud and fast and the plane shook and shuddered as we left the ground. I held Dad's hand tight and was just beginning to relax when there was a loud thump as the landing wheels were retracted into the plane. Now apparently everyone on board except me knew the thump noise was normal. Me however, thought the tail of the plane had hit the ground as we went up off the ground and I let out a loud scream. I'm sure the whole plane burst out laughing, sometimes I'm such a goose. Dad's laughter boomed out and he had tears running down his eyes. Glad I could provide him some "free" entertainment!

Despite the DVD player, the flight is long and boring and I eventually drift off to sleep. I awake to a bad smell, as much as I love Dad he eats too many baked beans and as a result often has a smelly gas problem. I try to ignore it and think of pleasant smells like maple syrup on pancakes, but it's no good I just have to say something. My, "Dad that's disgusting" comment comes out a bit too loud. The lady in front turns around and apologizes because her baby has pooped her nappy and she's just changing it. I don't know whose face went redder, mine or Dad's.

Finally we arrive and its soooooo HOT! Our apartment is lovely on the tenth floor with a lovely view of the ocean. The ocean is beautiful with bluish green water, dazzling white sand and the white water of the broken waves.

So lovely to look at, but Dad informs me he has booked me into a learn-to-surf lesson first thing tomorrow morning. I don't want to go into the ocean on a surfboard! Dad is big on trying new things and having new experiences. He thinks it helps you develop into a more confident person. Really...being pummeled by giant waves and chased by sharks is going to make me more confident.

Monday

Mom has hired a fluoro green helmet and a bright orange life jacket for my surf lesson. I think she is as horrified by the thought of me on a surfboard, out in the deep ocean, as much as I am.

I waddle over to the lift looking like an entrant in an extreme games competition. In the lift Dad lifts the helmet off my head and unties the life jacket and stuffs them into his backpack. With a smile and a Hawaiian hang loose gesture he says, "Lets just relax and enjoy the experience, but don't tell Mom."

Sometimes I think Dad is much cooler than Mom. Aaahh...well that is until I looked at his boardshorts. My eyes must have popped because Dad smiled and asked, "So, do you like my new surfie, hang ten, cool dude boardies?" I smiled back and told him that he looked like the coolest Dad in the world.

I'm great at the surf lesson. I paddle well, jump up on the board with ease, I can even walk down to the nose and hang ten with my toes. Then the instructor spoils it all by making us leave the sand and go into the water. The water is so warm, which is good because I'm spending a lot of my time falling into it. Being in the water on the board is very different, the board seems to have come alive, it moves to every bump and ripple in the ocean. When a wave comes it becomes an evil assassin, the board rips out of my hands and hits me in the head. Maybe that helmet wasn't such a bad idea after all. However persistence pays off and eventually I manage to stand up and ride a wave for a little while. The instructor gives me a friendly wave and hoot and I rush back out for another one. This is actually fun.

Thursday

After several lessons I'm getting much better and venturing much further out. I love sitting in the ocean, today there are some really good surfers doing tandem surfing. The guy takes off on the wave and then lifts his partner over his head, where she does all these gymnast type poses. They often all catch the same wave and glide along together. It looks fantastic! I'd love to be able to do that, maybe next holiday.

The next wave that rolls in has me paddling for it and five of these tandem surfers are paddling as well. I get up fast and start to glide along the wave, it's the biggest I've ever caught. I'm so excited because I know Mom and Dad are videoing this, my last surf. I can hear Dad's booming voice shouting, "Go Madonna." To my right I can see the tandems surfing alongside me. The pair next to me are incredible, he just swung his partner through his legs to the back of the board.

I should have been looking where I was going because suddenly I see another board floating by itself just in front of me (probably some uncool learner who can't stand up).

My board hits the loose board in the water and I fly airborne straight onto the tandem board next to me. Amazingly I land on my feet, but accidently push the tandem girl off her board. She disappears with a splash. But wait, it gets worse! The guy at the front (who is built like a giant) reaches back and grabs my hand. He pulls me closer and hoists me up into the air. This can't be happening! It is like I've turned into a bird flying in the air with absolutely no control. I waver back and forth and yell at him to "PUT ME DOWN!!!!"

Finally gravity wins and I topple to the right pulling my new partner with me. We take out the next surfing couple who continue to take out the next pair in a domino effect until all five tandem surfing couples are down in the water. Ten down. (Now if that was bowling, I'd have a great score.)

I finally struggle into shore, I feel as though the water must be evaporating around me from the redness of my embarrassed face, Mom goes, "That was great Madonna, and I got a great photo."

Monday

I Hate Bullies!

Back at school again and everything's great. I'm looking lightly tanned from my Hawaiian holiday and super fit. I have my Nike backpack, the one all the kids are envious of, with its orange and purple panels and the lime green inserts on the straps. I just love it!

I'm happily sitting in class next to my best friends, Gretel and Mr. Tall, Dark and Handsome when suddenly the Deputy Principal, Mrs. She Who Rules The School bursts in the door. "Who owns this bag," she snaps in her usual breaking glass voice. As I said, everyone loves that bag of mine. She must have seen it on the racks outside the classroom and been so impressed she just had to know which lucky student owned it. Funny how she is only holding it with one finger and at arm's length, almost as though she finds my bag distasteful in some way. When I raise my hand to claim ownership of the bag she instructs me to come with her. As I follow her out the door I wonder what those tiny white things are that seem to be falling off my bag.

When we get outside she snarls at me, "Don't you ever clean your bag," I start to reply, "Of course I do, look how clean…" When she lifts the flap, tips my bag upside down and starts to shake it. More of those tiny white things start to tumble out and they look like they are wriggling. Then something bigger falls out. It looks like someone has painted my sandwich bag green.

Oh no, I finally recognize the object, it's a meat sandwich I didn't finish eating at lunch time. Not today's lunch time, but lunch time a week ago - before my holiday. The green stuff is mould and those little white things are wriggling because they're maggots, flies have laid eggs in my rotten food and now maggots have hatched out.

After the last day of school I just threw my school bag in the corner without emptying it out. Mrs. She Who Rules The School leaves me to clean up my disgusting mess (as she calls it) while she rings my parents. I'm not sure what's worse getting all those wriggling maggots out of my bag or the laughter (and gasps of horror) as my class goes past on the way to the next lesson.

Finally Mom, Dad and I leave the school office after twenty minutes of lecturing from Mrs. She Who Rules The School about school standards and cleanliness. Mom fills in the trip home with her own version of the lecture. I don't think she likes maggots.

Tuesday

Ted Martin started calling me, 'Maggot' the next day, before too long some of the other sheep joined in. It wasn't unusual to hear, "Hey Maggot," called out to me five to six times on the way to class for the next week or two. But eventually people got sick of that joke and left it alone...except for Ted Martin.

Ted Martin was not terribly tall but had a permanent mean look on his face. His stocky muscular build and spiky haircut finished the image and most kids were scared of him. He was the type of bully that once he targeted you, he never let go. Ted needs a name and I decide to call him 'Pitbull'. It really suits him, not that I'd ever call him that to his face. I could see that Pitbull was going to be an ongoing problem for me, after all, how can I be a cool girl and try to fit in, when he keeps calling me Maggot.

Mr. TDH offered to tell Pitbull to back off for me, but I didn't want him to get into a fight and get hurt or in trouble. I should have just told the teachers but Pitbull was smart and never did it in front of any teachers and the other kids were too scared to speak against him. It would be hard to prove, it would be my friend's word against him and his friends. I'd have to solve this my own way.

Now Pitbull didn't just name call, he was quite versatile. He indulged in a bit of push and shove, tacks on your chair, throwing your bag into the bushes, taking your hat and pulling faces, but his specialty was taking your lunch. Daily he would stalk the eating area to select a victim who had a nice sandwich or even better a slice of chocolate cake. Pitbull would snatch the food away in a millisecond and laugh as he walked off.

Wednesday

I have hatched my plan to stop Pitbull calling me Maggot and maybe stop him from stealing lunches at the same time. Putting my recent experience with maggots to good use, I decided to create a little maggot farm, I carefully collected a few tasty left-overs and put them into a plastic lunch container with the lid off and left it in the backyard.

The Following Wednesday

After a week I had a nice colony of maggots and put the lid back on the container and then took it to school (carefully!!!! I didn't want another bag incident).

That lunchtime I waited patiently for Pitbull to prowl the eating area. I kept my slice of chocolate cake out of sight until just before the bell went. Then I start telling Gretel and Mr. TDH how lovely Mom's chocolate cake was (I used a loud voice), waving it around in front of them as I spoke.

As soon as I saw Pitbull approaching I quickly slipped it into the plastic lunch container (you know the lunch container I prepared at home). Pitbull reached for me just as the bell went and snatched the container right out of my hands. "Too late Maggot, I saw your chocolate cake, this will make a nice mid-class snack for me," he sneered, as he put the container in his pocket.

Pitbull often liked to keep some of his stolen food in his pockets and when the teachers weren't looking he would grab a quick bite. Pitbull sat in the middle of the room and I was several rows back. Our English teacher, who I preferred to call Mr. Albert because of his frizzy Albert Einstein hairdo, is giving a riveting lesson on nouns and verbs. However, my attention is focused on Pitbull. Halfway through the lesson I can see Pitbull starting to get restless and then he reaches into his pocket and I hear the snap of the lunch box lid being undone. Mr. Albert starts walking around the room as he talks and Pitbull quickly whips his hand out of his pocket. As I continue to watch I notice the little white maggots climbing up the side and along the back of his shirt. Soon Pitbull's back is a super highway for maggots as they escape the lunch container, some keep going up and some turn around and go down and some just go around in circles.

As Mr. Albert turns back to the board, Pitbull goes for a quick bite of the chocolate cake. Suddenly the room is rocked by the sound of coughing and spluttering as Pitbull realizes that he has a mouth full of chocolate cake and maggots!

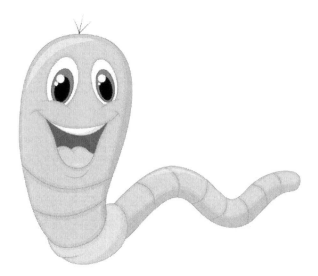

The coughing turns to vomiting as Mr. Albert escorts him from the room. Mr. Albert looks like he would like to vomit too. Double win! I don't think Pitbull will be calling me maggot anymore, in fact I'd be surprised if he ever uses the word maggot again. Hopefully he also thinks twice before stealing anyone's food again.

We were sent out of class early so that the mess can be

removed by the cleaners. Pitbull had to help them. Mrs. She Who Runs The School supervises us as we leave. She stares at me suspiciously, but I just give her a cheeky smile. Problem solved.

Thursday

Recreational Sport – Oh no...

Recreational Sport reads the note, put your name down for the sport of your choice. Unfortunately, Recreational Sport will be run on Fridays for six weeks. There are about six choices of sports including volleyball, skating and fishing but straight away my attention is grabbed by tenpin bowling. Air-conditioned, a takeaway food counter and music - now that sounds like my kind of sport. So I quickly put my name down.

Friday

The first week of tenpin bowling comes up fast and the supervising teacher is Mr. Eagle. I call him Mr. Eagle because of his bald head, the beady black eyes that just peer into your mind and the way he moves his head thrust slightly forward. Mr. Eagle swiftly forms us into groups for each alley. I end up in a group of four, which is good because you spend less time waiting. But bad because the group is Gretel, another girl called Sally, Pitbull and myself. That is just my bad luck, I can't believe that I managed to get stuck in his group!

This is a photo of Pitbull!

Ha ha, not really.

Since the maggot food incident, I wouldn't say Pitbull has been nice to me...but carefully neutral around me. Like Mrs. She Who Runs The School he suspects my involvement with his embarrassing maggot episode. I wouldn't say he is scared of me, just wary.

Pitbull bowls first of course! He doesn't so much bowl the ball, he actually hurls the ball down the alley. His run-up is so fast and his arm so powerful...it's a wonder the 10 pins don't shatter.

Then you have Sally, who is quite the opposite. She slowly walks out onto the alley, the ball seems almost too heavy for her and she nearly drags it on the ground. Sally releases the ball so slowly it just kind of meanders down the alley. It finally reaches the pins but doesn't knock any over, it just comes to a halt resting against them. After a few minutes one of the staff comes across and moves the ball and tells us to stop being silly and just bowl properly.

Gretel and I both managed to bowl a few balls down and I've even knocked some pins over. Meanwhile, Pitbull continues his frenzied attacks on the 10 pins sending them flying into the air each time. Eventually Pitbull can't help himself and starts making little snide comments about how weak we are and how our bowling "sucks". Of course, that annoys me and on my next turn I do a much faster run up and put all my strength into bowling that ball as fast as I can. It does go fast, the fastest I've ever bowled before. Unfortunately, I let go at the wrong time and my bowling ball isn't going down the alley but is heading backwards towards where the others are sitting. With a loud thump it lands on Pitbull's leg. He gives out an impressive shriek.

I race back to him apologizing, but he gives me his best mean stare. "You did that on purpose!" he yells at me. "Don't be silly," I reply, "I am not that accurate with my bowling."

While Pitbull limps over for his next go, I race over and buy a soft drink. I get back in time to quickly have my next go, making sure it goes down the alley this time. I sit down with my drink when I see that my five dollar bill has fallen out of my pocket and it is on the floor at the front of our alley. I race out to grab it as Pitbull selects his ball from the return rack. I'm in such a hurry I spill my drink on the floor. "Wait!" I yell to Pitbull, as I go to get a mop to wipe it up.

Pitbull generally doesn't listen to anyone and he certainly doesn't listen to me. As he goes to have his next bowl he goes even faster to make up for his limp (from my bowling ball). His feet hit my puddle of soft drink and Pitbull goes flying in the air. He goes so fast he continues to slide down the alley and his head hits the 10 pins - a strike actually, well done Pitbull. The attendant rushes to Pitbull's aid as the rest of the students clap. As Pitbull is helped up the alley to the seats, I tried to apologize again. He just looks at me and says, "Stay away from me!"

Buddy Class – How Cool!

"Everybody listen up," gushes Miss Learning Is Fun. "Today we have our first meeting with our year one buddy class and I have paired each one of you with a lovely grade one child, it's your job to be a responsible and sensible mentor. These little girls and boys will be shy and nervous around you big kids, so make sure you are extra nice with lots of warm smiles to make them feel welcome."

Little kids, I love little kids, so cute and adorable. How exciting to be a mentor, a big friend, to be able to reach across the years and offer a helping hand. I know, I know - I'm beginning to sound like my mother. But really this is going to be fantastic!

Miss Learning Is Fun walks us down to the year one building in the lower school. That's where we meet the year one teacher, Mrs. Jones who sounds like Miss Learning Is Fun magnified 10 times. Her enthusiasm is infectious and the two teachers quickly call out names to match us with a partner.

Gretel gets a cute little girl with pigtails in red bows. Mr. Tall Dark And Handsome gets a cute little boy with a huge smile. My buddy is called Dean, but he looks more like Dennis the Menace. Short, spiky red hair, a handful of freckles thrown across his face, a temporary snake tattoo on his arm and displaying a gap-toothed grin or smile (I'm not sure which). "That's an interesting tattoo," I say. "I like snakes," he replies, "they bite people." I don't know what to say to that, so I say nothing.

Our first buddy task is to color in a picture, with my artistic flair I'll soon have Dean and I creating a masterpiece. Except, Dean informs me in his cranky voice with a matching cranky face, that he doesn't like coloring and refuses to do the coloring sheet. I followed Miss Learning Is Fun's instructions and give him my big smile and using my nicest voice I offer to let him use my connector pens. This works a charm and a smile appears on his face. But my smile fades as Dean quickly puts my pens together to make a Star Wars sword and starts to hit Gretel and Mr. Tall Dark And Handsome with it. "Stop!" I yell and snatch the pens off him, putting them back on the desk.

Mrs. Learning Is Fun comes rushing over. "Madonna, remember you are a mentor, raising your voice like that is going to scare your buddy." I start to explain what he was doing when I realize that Dean is now quietly coloring the sheet. Miss Learning Is Fun gives me an unbelieving look and walks away. Dean just gives me a sly grin and alternates between coloring and sucking and chewing on my pens.

At last the picture is finished and I try to retrieve my pens from Dean. I got them all except my favorite pink colored one, that he continues to chew on. I try to yank it from his mouth, but because by now it is covered in slimy grade 1 boy saliva, it slips out of my hands and hits Miss Learning Is Fun in the back of the head. Great, I get another lecture about being a responsible mentor and threatened with detention.

The second activity involves us reading a simple book while the buddies follow the words with their fingers. It starts well, Dean does a great job for the first three pages but then I noticed his fingers have disappeared from the page. I look up from the book to see what he's doing. No wonder his fingers aren't following the words, he now has two of his fingers jammed far up his nose. As I watch the fingers reemerge from their mining expedition, they are now covered in green snot! Yuck! "Hang on Dean, I'll get you a tissue," I say. No need, Dean sticks his fingers into his mouth and starts chewing into an early lunch. I promptly turn around and vomit onto the reading book.

As Miss Learning Is Fun leads me down to the sick bay she says, "Now I know why you were not being a good mentor, you must be coming down with something." "I know you'll do a fantastic job next week when you get to work with Dean again." Miss Learning Is Fun thinks my groaning is because I feel sick, so she pats me on the shoulder. Next week for buddy time I think I'll bring a set of handcuffs and a bottle of disinfectant!

Dad's Surprise

I arrive home from school ready to kick back, grab a snack and maybe watch a little TV. My mellow mood is lost when I walk in and find Dad waiting for me with that smile on his face. You know that smile, the one your parents have when they've done something that they think is marvelous and in reality it's your worst nightmare.

He is hiding something behind his back. He brings his hands to the front revealing a hideous yellow shirt with a number on the back and some matching long black and yellow socks. I stare vacantly, still not getting it, when Dad announces he has signed me up for soccer.

The news only gets better! My first training session is on this afternoon. Now don't get me wrong, I think sport is great, to watch. I know playing sport helps you to be fit and healthy and sometimes I jog, but my coordination with ball sports isn't good. This is maybe because I have been very good at avoiding ball sports, it is surprising how easy it is to fake an injury or illness with a little Internet research.

We arrive at the soccer fields. Dad takes me across and introduces me to the coach, Mr. Cameron. Mr. Cameron introduces me to the rest of the team, about 14 kids. I'm glad to see the team includes four other girls. Mr. Cameron tells me just to call him Coach as that is what everybody else calls him. I must admit he is not what I expected, a towering mass of muscle yelling at the players. Coach isn't overly tall but looks fit, he seems to have a permanent smile on his face and a calm soft voice.

Coach tells us to all grab a soccer ball and jog around the field as a warm up. I'm keen to make a good impression so I quickly grab a ball and tuck it under my arm and take off first. I run hard and I'm the first back to coach. He gives me a smile and says, "Madonna when I said grab a ball, I meant get a ball and dribble it with your feet around the field, this is soccer we don't run and carry the ball." He told me to look at the others. I watched the rest of the team kicking the ball along as they run. Great first impression...how embarrassing!

We do lots more running and dribbling the ball and some passing with partners. Finally, coach calls us in for the last activity. He lines some balls up in front of the goal and instructs us to give one strong kick into the goal. I wisely head to the back of the line so I can watch and learn. The first few boys kick the ball straight into the goal and a few kick it too hard and send it way over the top of the goal. The other girls each kick it into the goal but not quite as hard as the boys. What a relief, this doesn't look too difficult at all.

Finally it is my turn, I get a good run up and swing my right leg as powerfully as I can. Stand clear everyone I think, here comes a Madonna missile. No missile, in fact the ball doesn't even move, my kick is a big air swing. I don't even touch the ball, but I do over balance and fall flat on my bottom.

The whole team erupts in laughter but coach quickly tells them to stop. "Have another go Madonna," he urges, "but this time come in a bit more slowly." I go back to the starting point and try again. This time I do connect with the ball. Unfortunately my boot just seems to slide off the side of the ball. The ball rolls to the left about a body length before stopping. This time the team is more controlled and doesn't burst into 'loud' laughter. I can still see some of their looks as they try to hold their laughter in.

When the training session ends coach calls me over. Perhaps I'll be saved and he'll dump me from the team. No such luck, he gives me a friendly smile and a few more tips. "One more thing Madonna, those shin pads are supposed to be worn under your socks and not on top of them." I hope he thinks my face is red from all the running around...not from the embarrassment of being such a kook.

Oh Boris!!!!

Boris the Bear sits at my student desk in my bedroom staring at me with those sad brown eyes. One eye is dangling down his cheek by a single thread. One ear is ripped off totally, a gaping hole in his stomach is leaking polyester stuffing and he's left foot is wet and fraying. A black tire tread mark is across his back. I've let everyone in my class down, they are all going to be so disappointed.

OOPS! REWIND! You will want to know how poor Boris the bear ended up like this. Who is Boris the Bear, well he is the property of Miss Learning Is Fun. She has had Boris since she was a little girl (which must be a very long time ago – she has to be at least 30).

Anyway, Miss Learning Is Fun had this great idea to help us with our writing. We each get to take Boris the Bear home and take photos of him in different situations. Then we bring them to school and the class can choose from one of the photos to write a story. It's something a bit different and everyone enjoys taking Boris home and trying to outdo each other in finding unusual places to photograph Boris.

That's when I had my great idea…I'd take Boris to the zoo and get some photos of him with a real bear.

So on Saturday I asked Mr. TDH and Gretel to come with me to the zoo. I borrowed Mom's camera and off we go. We decide to catch the bus to the zoo and we feel pretty grown up as we walked down to the bus stop. That is until I noticed little kids and adults giving me funny looks. You see, Boris the Bear is too big to fit into my bag so I'm carrying Boris in my arms like a baby. I guess a girl my age carrying a bear in public, isn't terribly cool.

I try and stick Boris under my jumper but this looks even stranger and he keeps falling out. Brain wave hits, I tuck

Boris under my belt at my back and my sweatshirt covers him. Problem solved and we quickly reach the bus stop. We only wait a few minutes before the bus arrives and we hop on. We choose the back seat and before I sit down...I reach back to remove Boris. Gone!!! Boris must have fallen out as I climbed onto the bus. In panic, I look out the back window as the bus pulls away. I spot Boris lying on the road just before the bus stop. Quickly we race to the front of the bus and ask the driver to stop and let us off. He says he can't let us off until the next official stop.

Five minutes later (okay – maybe only 2) and several kilometers (or a few hundred yards) further away we finally get off the bus. We run back and finally the original bus stop is in sight and I can still see Boris on the road. With relief I see that he appears unmarked until I look at his back and see the bus tire tread mark right across the middle. I tried to brush it off but it only slightly smudges, it is a mix of oil and road grime, no way it's coming off.

Mr. TDH, bless his heart, says, "Don't worry Madonna, it won't show up in the photos, you'll only see the front of Boris." I realize he is right, I can worry about cleaning it off later.

Finally we get to the zoo and all of us get distracted for a while looking at all the different animals. The tiger enclosure is fantastic with big glass panels (that are really thick – I hope), so you can see the tigers really clearly. Gretel suggests we just get photos of Boris with the Tigers in the background. But no, I insist on a bear photo and a check on the zoo map reveals a grizzly bear enclosure not far from where we are.

We quickly arrived at the grizzly bear enclosure, but we are disappointed to find it doesn't have glass viewing walls. Instead it has a high mesh wall that keeps us back from the steel bars of the main enclosure area. The mesh fence is going to be really hard to take pictures through, but then we spy a viewing platform that overlooks the enclosure and this will give us a clear picture above the mesh fence. I get Mr. TDH to hold Boris up with the enclosure in the background. But the real bear is too close to the front of the enclosure and I can't fit both the stuffed bear and the real bear in the photo. I instruct Mr. TDH to hold Boris the Bear out over the fence as far as he can and down lower. Mr. TDH looks a bit nervous but I tell him not to worry. But his hand is in the photo, so I tell him to just hold Boris by the tip of his ear. Mr. TDH reaches out and down and I start to line up the perfect shot. The grizzly bear lets out a huge roar and slams against the fence with a tremendous rattle. As he rips his hand back, Boris slips from his fingers and falls onto the top of the main fence and bounces into the bear enclosure.

Mr. TDH shrieks, I shriek louder, Gretel just shakes her head. I pass Gretel the camera and race down to the ground level closely followed by Mr. TDH. I can't see Boris in the enclosure, maybe he bounced back out. No! There he is in the real bear's paws! Grizzly lifts Boris up to his mouth and grabbed his left ear with his teeth. I hear a ripping noise as the ear is ripped from Boris's head. Boris falls to the ground and the bear pounces on him again. His jaw grasps Boris around the stomach, bits of stuffing go flying everywhere. The bear shakes Boris again and drops him to the ground. The grizzly is having a wonderful game with our class bear. He grabs him again, this time by the left foot and shakes his head from side to side wildly. Boris slips from the bear's mouth and goes flying. He lands halfway between the main bars of the enclosure and the mesh fence.

I race over and reach under the bottom of the mesh fence to try to get Boris. Grizzly does the same thing from his side of the enclosure. Fortunately grizzlies paw is too wide to get through the bars on the fence. But he doesn't give up and tries to dig under the fence to get to Boris. Mr. TDH stretches his arm under the fence. For one horrible moment Mr. TDH's hand actually touches one of the grizzly's paw. He snatches his hand back dragging Boris back. As the grizzly roars in frustration, we drag Boris out from under the fence.

We looked at each other, still a bit in shock and I realize not only is he tall, dark and handsome, but he's also my hero. Boris is torn and tattered but at least I have him back. Then Gretel comes charging down from the viewing platform with a great big grin on her face. "I got the best photos ever," she beams.

So that's why I'm sitting here in my bedroom with poor Boris the Bear looking so tattered and torn. I feel so bad, Miss Learning Is Fun will be so upset when she sees her childhood bear. The other kids in the class have grown so attached to Boris as well. I've let everyone down, but I'll just have to face the music and go and see Miss Learning Is Fun first thing in the morning.

I arrive at school early and hurry to Miss Learning Is Fun's room. As would be expected she's already setting up her class for the day's learning. She greets me with a smile and I blurt out how sorry I am for ruining her bear as I hold Boris out to her. Her face displays shock as her eyes take in the terrible damage Boris has suffered.

Then she looks back at me and smiles. "Don't worry Madonna," she says, "come into my office." I followed her in and watch in amazement as she opens a cupboard door to reveal three other immaculate Boris the Bears sitting inside. She pulls out one and replaces it with the tattered bear I have returned. "You see Madonna, every year one or two Boris the Bears don't survive the photo sessions, so I always keep some spares," smiles Miss Learning Is Fun. "But I thought Boris the Bear was your favorite childhood toy." "Yes Madonna he was, but my Boris the bear is a beautiful black and white panda bear, so no way was I letting a bunch of crazy kids put him in harms way. "The Boris legend just encourages the kids to take more care of the bear. Although, obviously not in your case. Gretel has emailed me your photos and I must say they are the best ever. Well done Madonna and remember the extra bears have to remain our little secret."

The Soccer Game

I sit bolt upright in bed as Dad's booming voice sings out, "We are the champions." "Come up Madonna, game day! Time to get up!" continues Dad.

Today is the day of my first soccer game. I'm glad Dad is excited because I'm terrified. I get dressed and on the way to the field Dad gives me a pregame pep talk. "Make every kick count, be first to the ball, push-up when you're defending," and a whole lot of other stuff which really made no sense to me at all.

On arriving at the field, I jog over to join the others who are gathering around the coach. I notice the other team at the opposite end of the field. They look like they had cornflakes and steroids for breakfast. A few of my teammates also look nervously at our opponents. The coach picks up on our nervous looks and admits the other team is big, fast and very good. He also reminds us that winning isn't everything and the important thing is to play our best and enjoy the game. I love our coach. "Remember," he says, "you didn't join the team to win games, you joined because you like playing soccer." Hang on, I only joined because Dad signed me up. Anyway, knowing that coach isn't going to be upset with us if we lose, takes some of the nerves away.

Coach shows us his game plan and assigns us playing positions. He makes me a left mid-fielder. When I ask which left, he looks at me strangely for a while then walks me to the other side of the field and shows me where to stand.

Soon the referee blows his whistle and we run onto the field and shake hands with the other team. So far...so good. I take my position and while waiting for the game to start, I glance at the sideline. Great news, standing alongside Dad and Mom are Gretel and Mr. TDH. Mom must have brought them along to watch me play. Dad spots me looking and gives a booming, "Go Madonna!" How embarrassing!

The referee blows the whistle and the game starts. I stand in my position and watch as the other team constantly attacks down the opposite side scoring several goals. So far the ball has come nowhere near me, but rolls past just out of my reach. That happened another three times and each time I watch it roll past. I'm beginning to wonder if the coach told me to stand in the wrong spot. Finally the referee signals half time and we jog off the field for a drink.

Coach calls me aside, "Madonna," he patiently explains, "when I showed you where to stand I didn't mean you couldn't move, that's just where to stand at the start of the game. You can move around to get the ball when it comes near your side of the field." "Okay," I reply, as my face turns a beetroot red color.

Soon half time is over and we are called back onto the field. Dad starts giving some cheerleader type calls, "M.A.D.O.N.N.A – Go Madonna!" He uses his earsplitting loudest possible voice. I notice that one of the attacking forwards in the other team is a very athletic looking girl with pigtails. As she sprints past me for the third time, I comment that I like her hair. She looks at me in confusion and stumbles into me and trips over.

The referee blows the whistle and gives me a yellow card (which apparently is a warning of rough play and if I get another one it becomes a red card and I get kicked out of the game). I tried to explain that I didn't trip her but he waves me away. I offer my hand to help the girl to her feet and notice she is wearing a lovely bright pink mouth guard. I remind myself to get one of those for the next game.

Meanwhile Mr. Boom Boom (my Dad) is going ballistic, over

the referee giving me the yellow card. Until Mom tells him to be quiet. The game recommences and the other team score another goal off the free kick. On the kickoff, the ball somehow ends up at my feet. Remembering everything coach has taught me I kick it as hard as I can and it goes flying down the field. Well if I thought Dad had been loud before, now it was on the 10 out of 10 scale. "Go Madonna, that's my daughter!" And then he starts the Madonna chant again. Suddenly the referee blows his whistle to stop the game and strides angrily over to my Dad on the sideline. I can't hear everything the referee says, but the main point is that Dad has to be quiet because the players can't hear his whistle and his instructions. "Be quiet or leave the grounds!" yells the referee.

That's my Dad...how embarrassing. I notice that Mom, Gretel and Mr. TDH have all shuffled along a bit from my Dad.

The game restarts and I get a few more kicks and dad manages to stay reasonably quiet. The girl with the pigtails gets past me several times to score more goals. The coach gets one of the other players, Mary, to drop back to help me to defend against her attacking runs.

Miss Piggy Tails starts another run aiming to get past me, but Mary shoulder charges her and this sends her crashing to the ground. Mary heads off with the ball. As everyone else heads off in pursuit of the ball, I noticed that Miss Piggy Tails hasn't got back up and is lying quite still on the ground. I rush over to her and squat down to check on her. She is going blue in the face and making strange noises. By now the referee has noticed and has stopped the game and rushes over. The referee and the rest of the team have gathered around. I notice half her lovely pink mouth guard lying next to her head. Then it dawns on me that she is choking. I open her mouth and reach in and feel around. My fingers brush against the other end of the mouth guard, so I grab it and try to pull it out, but it's stuck firmly in her throat, I pull harder and it pops out of her mouth. Miss Piggy Tails gives a giant gasp and sits up, sucking in air in huge gulps.

Just then the paramedics arrive, they quickly check her over and the referee tells them what I did. One of the paramedics turns to me and says, "Well done young lady, you saved her life."

Some of the other players run back to their parents on the sideline. I stand in shock, watching Miss Piggy Tails talking to the paramedics. She is helped off and I slowly walk over to my family. As I approach the sideline the spectators from both teams start to clap. Dad's voice booms out, "Three cheers for Madonna!" As the cheers die down, I reach Mom and Dad. They each give me a big cuddle and a kiss. People gather around and pat me on the back. Then Gretel gives me a big hug and whispers, "You are fantastic." Mr. TDH also gives me a hug and tells me that I'm a hero. Me...a hero! Is this a dream? I LOVE SOCCER! And I LOVE my new school!

Maddi

Story 3 - Meet the Cousins

Wednesday – New Year's Eve

Boom, another flash rips apart the dark of the night sky. The sounds are deafening and the exploding colors sear your eyeballs. My heart pounds like a drum in my chest while my companion lies under my bed, his tongue hangs out of his mouth as he pants loudly. Finally the explosions finish. That's it, the end, Madonna Bull (that's me) has officially survived another year.

A bit embarrassing greeting the start of a new year hiding under the
blankets, but I've always found the fireworks on New Years Eve really scary. So when Dad…I call him Mr. Boom Boom because of his ear destroying loud voice…bought some fireworks to put on his own private display, I knew I was in for a wild night. (A new reason to call him Mr. Boom Boom!)

Fortunately I'm not the only one in the family scared of fireworks, so is Tyson, our family's pet Great Dane. Tyson joined me when I snuck back upstairs and hid in my bedroom. Girl and dog turned into chickens by a few fireworks.

I'm a little sad the year is over, I've had such a great year. I moved to Harper Valley School, made some great friends like Gretel and the dreamy Richard Jones or as I call him Mr. Tall Dark and Handsome. My Mom and Dad got back together after a brief separation and I learnt to play soccer.

As silence descends the house, a beaming Mr. Boom Boom calls us altogether. "I've got some exciting news," he starts. When my Dad is enthusiastic, his voice gets even louder! "We're going on a holiday to Australia to meet your Uncle Jim, Aunty Jill and your two cousins."

AUSTRALIA – wow, for once Dad is on a winner, Australia sounds so exciting! But Uncle Jim and Aunty Jill are just a mystery to me. Aunty Jill is Dad's sister, I've only met her once before when she visited us for a week. I was only young, but from memory she was a female version of Dad…booming voice and tall and imposing like Dad. I've never met Uncle Jim or their two children, my cousins. This certainly sounds like an interesting trip.

When Dad makes a decision he acts on it fast! "We leave in TWO days!" he announces.

Friday

The house is frantic as we plan and pack. I carefully pack all my best clothes into two bags before Mom bursts into the room to help me. I call her Mrs. Absolutely Positive because she always sees the positive side of things. Really she is a hippy alternative type of mom. She's great and I love her so much, but sometimes a kid can only take so much positivity!

This trip seems to be stressing Mom out. I don't get her normal everything will be fine smile, instead I get, "You can't take that much luggage," yell. "One bag!" Just call me one bag Madonna. Sadly I cut back my clothes to one bag, but then I have a brainwave…on the day we leave I'll just wear more than one outfit, brilliant!

Saturday

On the morning we leave we have to drop Tyson at the *Doggie Vacation Resort.* It doesn't look like a resort to me! I don't think it looks like a resort to Tyson either! I feel sad to leave Tyson, but a Great Dane on a plane just isn't going to work for anyone. It's my job to lead him in to the resort. He looks at me with those big puppy dog eyes and I feel like a traitor. I give Tyson one of his favorite dog biscuits and a big cuddle. Dad and I both have tears in our eyes as we leave, but I know Tyson will be safe and we'll see him soon.

I've managed to squirm into 3 tops, but they are all different colors and styles and it looks pretty silly. So I put a long sleeved white shirt over the top of them. I even manage to get two pairs of long pants on too. Yes, I move very stiffly. Yes, I look like an overinflated version of myself. But at least some of my favorite clothes from my second bag will get to come on holiday with me.

We arrive at the airport and after about an hour we finally are all checked-in and waiting to get on the plane. The call is made to board the plane and together we head up the passage way to the plane door. With all those clothes on, I have a definite waddle going on. I can barely keep up with my parents and I overhear Dad whisper to my Mom, "I think we had better cut down on treats for Maddi."

At the entrance to the plane awaits the beautiful, smiling hostess...perfect hair, perfect uniform and of course...a perfect smile. I think her name is obvious – Miss Perfect! That's until I reach the entrance, then the perfect smile slips into an "oh" of surprise and then a quiet laugh. "Well with a shirt like that you won't have to worry about spilling your food on yourself," the perfect girl in the perfect uniform laughs. Miss Perfect is being quite rude.

Then I follow her eyes and look down at my shirt. Tyson! Great Danes are incredible dogs, big legs, big tails, big heads and very big mouths that unfortunately make very big spit messes. That goodbye cuddle with Tyson has left my shirt covered in a lovely mix of dog spit, dog hair and a half-chewed dog biscuit.

I ask Mom and Dad why they didn't tell me. They just smile and reply that we didn't have time to go back to get another shirt. I'm wearing three other shirts! But they didn't know that and I couldn't tell them that I had all those clothes on (that I was told NOT to bring). I guess that's why they say…honesty is the best policy.

Once we take off, Miss Perfect redeems herself by bringing a hot wet towel and helping me to clean up my shirt.

Sometimes I think my family is a little strange, but as I sit in my seat on the plane I realize I'm definitely right. There's my

Mom on the other side of the aisle listening to some music with those headphones they provide on the plane. Seems harmless enough until she starts to sing along with the song out loud. Mom has many amazing talents, unfortunately singing isn't one of them! Her badly off-tone voice screeches out as she happily sings along with the range of rock songs…but my personal favorite is Mom's version of We Will Rock You.

It's my favorite because the ever-smiling Miss Perfect has forgotten her perfect smile as she taps Mom on the arm to get her attention. "Excuse me, can we please ask you to stop singing," she asks in her pleasant voice. "What!" yells Mom, "speak up, I can't hear you!" Isn't it funny when people with headphones on can't hear you…they seem to forget they can just take them off and they yell as if everyone else can't hear.

Miss Perfect's perfection is slipping away, she yanks the headphones off Mom's head and snarls, "Can you please stop that awful singing, you are annoying the whole plane."

That's when my Mom – Mrs. Absolutely Positive – lives up to her name. "Oh sorry dear, well at least I gave everyone something to talk about, these long plane trips can be so boring," she replies with a smile and a wink.

Miss Perfect tries to return the smile, but not with much warmth and I notice she keeps the headphones in her hand as she walks away down the isle.

I turn to Dad to smile at him about the "singing" incident, but he has fallen asleep. Oh NO, I cringe. I call Dad, Mr. Boom Boom because of his earth-shattering voice…but when Dad falls asleep his ability to make enormous noises continues. Dad's snoring is just beginning, but from experience I know it will only grow in volume as he goes into a deeper sleep.

I decide to wake him up, but I don't want him to know it was me or he'll be grumpy all flight. I try giving him a nudge with my elbow, but he doesn't even quiver. I flick his ear with my finger, he turns his head but there is no sign of awakening. The snoring starts to get louder. Finally in desperation, I lift his eyelid revealing a blood-shot eye slightly rolled back in his head. Gross! But he is still fast asleep.

There is only one thing to do, give up! I take out my set of headphones, crank up the volume and start to enjoy the music. I tap the beat to the music on the armrest of the chair…but take care NOT to sing. I don't want to sound like my mother.

I'm really relaxed and enjoying the music with my chair back and my eyes closed when I feel a very insistent tapping on my arm. My eyes spring open to find Miss Perfect kneeling down in the aisle next to my seat. "Excuse me," she says, "is that your father making that dreadful noise? Is he okay, or is this some kind of medical emergency?"

"Yes he's my father," I reply. Mom leans across the isle and butts in, "He's my husband too."

"Of course he is," replies Miss Perfect, "I should have realized," she says in a strange tone of voice. I tell her that Dad is okay, he is just a loud snorer.

"Well dear, you'll just have to wake him up, he is disturbing the whole plane," she quietly snaps. I'm beginning to think she doesn't like our family.

I try the tap on the arm, the shake of the shoulder, even the elbow in the ribs, but Dad barely stirs. He's like a bear in hibernation for the winter. That's when I get my brilliant idea. I've got one of those plastic drinking cups that they serve your drinks in on the plane. I've finished the drink, but the ice cubes are still in the cup. Dad is still thundering away, Miss Perfect is at the other end of the aisle glaring at us and coming our way. Desperate times call for desperate measures! I pull Dad's shirt out from his neck and tip the ice cubes down the front of his shirt. That works! Dad comes awake with a bellow, tries to jump up from his seat, but the belt jerks him back down. He crazily starts trying to flick the ice out from his shirt and this sends the ice cubes flying in all directions.

Some of the flying ice missiles hit human targets...the passengers in front of us! Some even manage to slip down their shirt and dress fronts and before you know it, four other people are jumping up in their seats making strange noises as the ice cubes slide down against their skin.

Mom starts laughing hysterically! Dad joins in with his booming laugh and I just try to shrink into the chair.

Miss Perfect comes storming down the isle. With her perfectly false smile she quietly snarls, "Keep the noise down or I'll leave the **Keep Seat-belts Fastened** sign on for the whole flight."

Yes, that's my family, they have turned Miss Perfect into a rabid monster and we are only half way through the flight. Mom and Dad wink at me and we all sit back and settle down, just like a "normal" family.

Finally the flight arrives in Sydney. The view from the plane was awesome! I whip out my polaroid camera and take my first photo of Australia.

Sunday (Australian time)

We collect our hand luggage and shuffle along the aisle.
There is no sight
of Miss Perfect as we depart the plane, after dealing with our
family she is probably busy looking for another
job...something more relaxing like being a crocodile handler
or a test crash dummy!

After we get through customs, we head into the main part of
the airport to meet up with our relatives. The airport is
FULL of people and we gaze around looking for Aunty Jill,
when suddenly I hear this booming female voice, "Hey
Bully, I'm over here!" It's Dad's sister, Aunty Jill. Oh my
gosh, she sounds just like Dad, only a bit more girly – scary!

Aunty Jill is very different to my Mom, her face is very
made-up with copious amounts of make-up and very short
blonde hair that is so stiff it doesn't move. Not even a single
hair!

Aunty Jill herds us out to the car park and we jump into her
big 4-wheel drive. She explains that Uncle Jim and our two
cousins, Jenny and Jack are waiting at the units where we
are staying. We'll be there for a couple of days before we
head north up the coastline.

Jill, Jim, Jenny and Jack...what is it with this family...with all
those J names. I've only met Aunty Jill once before when I
was very young, so I'm watching and listening to her
carefully, to get an impression of what she's like. I've got one
word that describes her quite well. Bossy! And even in the
wind, her hair does not move at all.

A lot of her sentences start with...you should. You should go
to bed early tonight. You should get something to eat at the

Chinese restaurant over the road from the units. You should go for a Sydney Bridge Walk.

Mom mentions that she would really like to visit Bondi Beach because it looks so beautiful. Mom has seen a show about Bondi and it is on her "to do" list.

"You shouldn't worry about going to Bondi," booms Aunty Jill, "seen one beach and you've seen them all, you'll see plenty of beaches on our road trip." Mom gives her a strained smile, come on Mrs. Absolutely Positive, you can do better than that!

When we go up to the units we find that although they are separate units, they have a door that is unlocked and lets you go from one unit to the other. We are quickly introduced to Uncle Jim. He is tall, sun-tanned and seems quite nice. Not quite as "intense" as his wife.

I also get to meet my cousins, Jenny and Jack. Jenny is the same age as me, while Jack is about three years younger.

Of course Aunty Jill says, "**You should** get to know each other." She shuffles us into the other unit. Awkward!!!! For what seems like a VERY long moment, we stare at each other. Jenny is stunningly beautiful with brown eyes and brown hair that falls to the middle of her back and whiter than white teeth.

Jack looks very different with reddish sandy colored hair.

We exchange a few strained greetings as we eye each other up and down. "Your hair is so beautiful," I blurt out to Jenny. "I know," she replies.

"And you're so cute," I continue to Jack. "Yes," he replies.

Okay, mental note, modesty isn't a highly valued quality in this family. Jenny re-enforces this idea with her next statement, "I have an IQ of 148 and had to skip two year levels at school because I'm so smart. Also I've been Dux every year that I've attended school."

"That's um, nice," I reply, while thinking how Brains will be a great nickname for Jenny. "How about you Jack?" I ask, "I suppose you are in your final year about to graduate as a doctor," I continue sarcastically.

"Of course not!" snaps Brains, "he takes after Dad, I'm the brainy one in the family." Then she spends the next ten minutes quizzing me on a mix of questions about Math, English and Science stuff that I have never heard of.

We have just established that Brains is a genius and I'm NOT when Mom comes in to take us all to lunch. Thanks for the SAVE Mom!!!

After lunch Brains and I are told by Mrs. Bossy, "You should take Jack up to the roof top garden and admire the view."

The rooftop is amazing, the view of the harbor is beautiful! The bridge over the river is huge and very high. Along the top of the bridge I can see little figures that look like they're moving. When I ask what's that on top of the bridge, Jack tells me that it's people doing the bridge walk. "It's going to be so much fun when we do it tomorrow," he gushes.

I feel a moment of panic and I just hope that "we" doesn't include me! Anyway, it isn't until tomorrow, I'll have plenty of time to think of an excuse not to go.

I then decide to go and get my camera from the unit so I can take some photos. I leave the other two on the roof and head for the lift. I press the button and wait and wait and wait! Then I see the door leading to the stairway. It's only a 10 storey building and our unit is on the 8th floor. I decide to take the stairs rather than wait for the lift. I hurriedly rush into the stairwell and get down about five steps before I hear the heavy metal stairway door clang shut. I get a bad feeling as I walk back to the door and try the handle...LOCKED! Uh oh! I try knocking but the door is so thick I hardly make any noise. No noise...no way Brains and Jack are going to hear me. I decide I'll just walk down the stairs to the next floor and hope the door isn't locked. Three flights further down and still no unlocked doors.

Now I'm getting worried. Each floor further down seems to be getting darker, dirtier and scarier with graffiti on the walls. No one knows where I am and if I can't find a way out, who knows how long I'll be stuck in here. I think I'm on the third floor and my legs are on fire from walking down all those flights of stairs when I finally find an unlocked door.

With a loud squeal the door opens into a large office. It's Sunday, so nobody is there, but luckily for me there are some lights on, so I can see where I'm going. At the far side of the room I can see a lift door that I head straight for. Halfway there I have an awful thought…what if the office has some type of motion sensor and I set off an alarm. I freeze. I remember seeing a spy film where the spy crawled along the floor underneath the beams of the motion sensors. I'll look really really silly but who cares, nobody will see. I drop down to the carpet and start to crawl to the lift.

Then a thought stops me again. Security cameras! I pull my shirt over my head and continue to crawl to the lift. Crawling is SO much slower than walking and I'm getting carpet burns on my knees and elbows. However it is better than risking setting off an alarm and getting arrested.

I reach the lift and pray that it doesn't need a special card to make it open and work. It doesn't and I finally relax as it starts the climb to the 8th floor. I forget about going back up to the roof with my camera and instead I grab some ice from the fridge for my carpet burns. When Mom asks me what happened, I decide that admitting to being trapped in the stairwell is just way too embarrassing, so I just tell her that I tripped coming out of the lift.

After dinner, Mrs. Bossy (Aunty Jill) decides we should all go out and get some ice cream for dessert. My legs are still killing me, so I use sore knees as an excuse not to go.

As the rest of the family leave the unit…the news comes on.
Doesn't matter where you live in the world, the news is
BORING! And then the next story comes on, it is about a
mysterious burglar who broke into an office building in a
high-rise resort building in Sydney. They show some poor
quality black and white video of someone crawling along the
floor with a shirt pulled over their head. I stopped breathing.
Sweat poured out of my hands. The policeman was talking
(focus Maddi – what is he saying!). "…nothing has been
stolen, at this stage we think the suspect is a young teenager
and it may be a kid's prank, but we are continuing our
investigation."

Phew, I breathe a sigh of relief. Thank goodness the rest of
the family is downstairs getting an ice cream! I quickly race
into my bedroom and change my clothes. They go to the
bottom of my bag and that is where they will stay until we
get home! Close call!!!!

Monday

The next morning my peaceful sleep is shattered by the booming sound of Mrs. Bossy's voice, calling rise and shine. I try to ignore her as I figure she must be talking to the sun as it is still dark and the sun hasn't risen yet. But as the blanket if ripped off me, I realize I'm included. As the whole family assembles in the pre-dawn darkness, Mrs. Bossy starts reading off a list she has made.

4:45am leave for bridge
5:00am commence bridge walk
7:00am finish bridge walk
7:05am breakfast
7:15am walk to Ferry Terminal
8:00am catch the ferry to Manly
and so on…

True to her list we are at the base of the bridge at 5:00am, getting ready for the walk in the pre-dawn darkness.

Dad looks like he is sleep walking, his eyes are almost closed and his yawns are so big I can see his tonsils! Mr. Boom Boom is very quiet. He doesn't normally get up until at least 7am! I take after my Dad, I don't do mornings well.

While my Mom, Mrs. Absolutely Positive is living up to her name. "How exciting, we'll be able to watch the sun rise from the bridge." She is all perky and excited.

Before we can start the bridge walk we have to listen to a safety talk. My fear of heights wakes me up instantly and I carefully listen. I feel a bit more relaxed knowing we each are clipped onto a safety rail for the whole walk.

Then we are each given a set of brown overalls to put over our clothes. Apparently bridge walkers have no fashion sense.

Finally we get going and at the start it is fine. We walk in a line and as we come onto the metal walkway that leads to the top of the bridge, our guides clip our safety lines on. The higher we climb, the worse I feel, I'm trembling so much I can barely make my feet move as we reach the very top of the bridge. Mom and Dad rave about the view and I must admit…when I stop chanting – "don't look down, don't look down" – and I take a peek, it is spectacular! But a quick look down sends my head spinning!

Did I mention the wind? It's blowing a gale and the higher we go the windier it becomes. As Uncle Jim said, "It's windy enough to blow the fleas off a dog." This must be some strange Aussie saying. ☺

Then Mom decides to take a photo of Dad and me. Brown overalls, pale freezing and sick looking face and my hair is a tangle of knots, let's just say not one of my best photos! Mom shows me how she has loaded it onto her Facebook page. "I tagged you Maddi, so all your friends can see what a great time you are having," she says in a proud voice. "Thanks Mom," I reply. I'll get rid of the tag when we get back to the unit.

We continue the walk and finally reach the ground on the other side. I maintain some coolness and stop myself from getting down and kissing the ground. I smile and nod as Brains and Jack go on and on about how amazing the walk was.

We follow Mrs. Bossy's timetable and go to breakfast. I have yummy bacon and eggs and then I eat half of Mom's pancakes as she is too full. The only downside to breakfast is surviving another of Brain's pop quizzes, she just wants to make sure that I remember that she is a genius.

Then we walk down to the Ferry Terminal. I have no idea what a ferry is. In my early morning haze I am imagining little fairies flying around, you know, like the tooth fairy. But a ferry is a large old wooden boat.

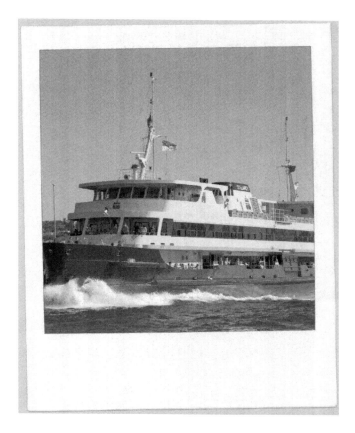

We quickly board the old boat and it sets off across the harbor for Manly beach. As we chug along, a new streamline hydrofoil boat speeds past us. "That's one of the newer boats," scoffed Mrs. Bossy, "they have absolutely no character and you can't feel the movement of the ocean beneath you." It looks pretty nice to me!

As a surprise our ferry actually stops at Luna Park first. Luna Park is an old amusement park with some old style rides.

We have a lot of fun there, even Brains seems to smile a bit more…after she explains to me how centripetal force worked. Ho Hum!

Just before we leave to go back on the ferry I buy some cotton candy (they call it fairy floss here). It was so yum, I finished it off really quickly. I can beat Brains at some things!

As the ferry heads across the bay we hit a few waves and my

stomach begins to churn. As the trip goes on, my stomach grows worse and worse. I start to look for the toilet just in case. I find it! It is just behind the 'Out of Order' sign. Oh no, the rocking of the boat is getting worse as is the rumbling of my stomach. The wind I felt up on the bridge was nearly as strong down here on the water. Things in my stomach department are now getting desperate. I wish I hadn't eaten so much for breakfast or all that cotton candy.

I looked around for Mom and see that she and Mrs. Bossy are standing at the railing at the front of the boat. I race over to Mom and squeeze in between her and Mrs. Bossy. Too late! As I start to tell Mom that I think I am going to be sick, I feel a surge of vomit come into my throat. I do the only thing I could do and lean over the railing, letting it erupt out of my mouth. The strange things you notice in situations like these, as the vomit spews from my mouth I admire its pretty pink color.

On a less windy day it would have been fine, going over the side of the boat into the water below, but not today. That wind is so strong. So strong that it blows the pink colored vomit back onboard. Some flecks hit my face, but the vast majority flies back straight into Mrs. Bossy's face. As bits of my breakfast drip off her face I can't help but think that her makeup and hairdo are ruined for the day. Mom wipes Mrs. Bossy's face off with some tissues as best she can. With her face devoid of makeup and her hair a tangled mess of curls, Mrs. Bossy looks very different. She wants to go home but Uncle Jim pats her on the back, "Don't worry. She'll be right mate." Another Aussie saying???

So we get off at Manly and have a lovely lunch—I don't feel sick once I get off the ferry. Uncle Jim buys some ginger candy for me to chew so I won't get sick on the return trip. The beach looks beautiful and we have fun splashing in the shallows. On the return ferry trip Mrs. Bossy stays well away from me.

It's a bit embarrassing to talk about but since we've arrived in Sydney my toilet trips have been ahh—difficult. I finally tell Mom and she explains that sometimes when you travel and eat food you're not used to, your bowels can get clogged up. She buys me a bag of prunes and says if I eat some of them it should help me. If a few prunes will help, the whole bag should fix me straight away! Maybe Brains isn't the only genius after all.

Tuesday

Today we leave Sydney to head up north along the coast.
Mom and Dad have hired a small car to go in, but once Dad
has loaded up the luggage the little car is looking pretty
crowded. That's when Aunty Jill utters those faithful words,
"Madonna **you should** go in our car, we've got a lot more
room." In my mind I scream "NO!" in reality I just nod with
an, "Oh." Eight hours trapped in a car with Brains giving me
quizzes, little Jack perfecting the art of being the annoying
younger brother and Mrs. Bossy giving me the entire 'you
should' range from careers to hair styles.

I'm about to climb into the car when Uncle Jim calls out,
"Hang on little mate," I freeze with my hand on the door
handle and to my amazement Uncle Jim pulls out one of
those mini battery powered vacuum cleaners and gives my
shoes a quick vacuum over before he lets me in the car. He
does everyone else's feet as well. Brains looks at me with a
sorry smile on her face and says, "You'll have to forgive
Dad, he just loves his car."

We are heading to a place called Sandy River National Park,
which I admit sounds nice but is unfortunately about eight
hours drive away. Sometime after the first hour my stomach
starts to rumble and grumble. At first it's not that loud but
the volume grows as time goes on. Soon both Brains and
Jack are obviously hearing my stomach as they both start to
give me some strange looks. It gets worse, it was that big bag
of prunes. I've gone past the stomach noises, now VERY,
VERY smelly farts are escaping me. Brains winds down her
windows and sticks her head halfway out, while Jack just
pinches his nose shut with his fingers and wiggles around
on his seat.

Eventually the smells reach Uncle Jim and Aunt Jill, I hear

some groans and whispered conversation. Uncle Jim calls out asking if anyone needs the toilet. How embarrassing! I try to build up my courage to admit I do when Jack beats me to it. He yells out, "Madonna needs to go, real bad!"

By the time Uncle Jim finds a toilet to stop at, I'm at the desperate stage. As soon as the car stops I'm out the door, bolting for the toilet. I make it, but only just and have to spend more minutes sitting on the toilet than a civilized person ever should.

Finally, I'm able to return to the car, everyone is out walking around, stretching their legs. Except for Uncle Jim who is emptying a can of air freshener into the car interior. As we climb back into the car to continue the journey the lemon smell is a bit over-powering but not as bad as the *"Madonna on prunes"* smell.

We eventually catch up with Mom and Dad when they stop for lunch at a little roadside seafood cafe. Mom and Dad order a big pile of prawns (we call them shrimp in America) and we all sit down at the table to eat. Now I've never eaten prawns before but I am starving so I grab one and shove it in my mouth and start chewing. It is TERRIBLE all crunchy shell with sharp edges. It is so bad I grab a napkin and spit it out of my mouth. As I take the napkin away from my mouth I realize everyone is looking at me and laughing.
"Madonna," Mom manages to gasp out between her bouts of laughter, "you have to peel the shell off the prawn before you eat them." The second prawn tastes much better.

After lunch it was only about three more hours before we reach Sandy River. Dad loves to stay in units when we go on holidays while Mom loves to camp. One look at Sandy River National Park lets me know that this is definitely the camping section of our holiday. Sandy River has a river, a beach, lots of trees, some flat grassy areas, a brick fireplace and an old wooden building. I assume that it must be the toilets and showers. Mom's in her element and starts using phrases like "being one with nature" and "discovering the great outdoors".

Aunt Jill and Uncle Jim pull out three tents from their boot, so the parent couples have one tent each and me and the dynamic duo share the other one. Of course our tent has no instructions, so we have to figure out how to put it up by watching the adults. Dad was going to help us until Mrs. Bossy yelled out, "No Bully, they need to learn to be self-sufficient!"

After a long hot hour, I learnt two things: how to put up a tent and that having an IQ of 148 doesn't mean you know how to put up a tent. Luckily Jack and I were able to figure out where to put the poles and how to peg the tent down, whilst Brains just didn't get it.

Eventually the tent was up. A bit lopsided and a bit wobbly, but we had somewhere to sleep. Jack and I get along surprisingly well and Brains even thanks me for all my help. Maybe this holiday might be more fun that I thought.

With the tent up, my thoughts turn to the toilet again. NO PRUNES EVER FOR ME AGAIN!!!!!!! As I head off to the toilet, Jack calls out, "Don't look down!" with a laugh. A strange thing to say, I think to myself as I reach to open the toilet door. The sign reads...**Pit Toilet**.

When I open the door the smell is terrible, but my need is so great that I HAVE to go in. Giant blowflies buzz around, the toilet seat looks normal (well, kind of normal – it is pink!), but I can't find any buttons to press to flush the toilet.

As I go to sit on the toilet seat…I look down into the toilet bowl. Now I understand! Now I know why Jack said don't look down. This toilet doesn't have a normal bowl, what you do in the toilet just drops into a big hole underneath, a giant pit! Guess that is why they call it a pit toilet. In the gloom of the pit I can see and SMELL what has been done by whoever went before me. Actually I can see what was done by many people who went before me! GROSS!!!!! I hold my breath, finish my business and get out of there as fast as I can.

Back at the tent…Jack, Brains and I do some bonding over how gross the toilet is. I'm feeling pretty tired and dirty and I ask them where the showers are. They smile and point towards the beach. "Do you wash in the ocean?" I ask. "No Maddi, explains Jack, there's a pipe sticking out of the sand dune with fresh water from an underground spring, the water constantly flows from the pipe.

"How do you shower in the open, people will see me," I say in a horrified voice. "You wear your bikini, this is real camping," replies Jack.

I walk down to the beach with my bikinis on and my toiletry bag, hoping that the pipe shower is just a joke. No joke! There sticking out of the sand hill about 3 meters above me is a rusty pipe. Flowing out of the pipe is a torrent of water, at least the water is clean and clear. I grab my shampoo and soap and jump under the water to discover it is FREEZING cold! Mom would be proud, I set a new World Record for the fastest shower ever and then sprint back to our tent to change into my clothes.

That night we have dinner cooked on a BBQ and afterwards we sit round the fire. Uncle Jim pulls out a guitar and we sing along with him. Camping is fun. The night is clear, the stars are bright and there is a huge full moon shining down on us.

We have the whole campground to ourselves. I think all the other campers have gone to the campgrounds that have real toilets and hot showers!

Eventually Mrs. Bossy says we should all go to bed as she has a big day planned for tomorrow. I'm still a bit hungry so I grab a loaf of bread out of the car and eat a few slices. I'm too tired to bother taking the bread back to the car, so I just leave it on the table with our plates and cutlery.

Sometime in the middle of the night, I wake up to a rustling sound. The full moon is shining brightly through our tent window and I can see that both Brains and Jack are sound asleep. The rustling sound is coming from just outside our tent. Then I hear the plates being knocked off the table. Someone is stealing our stuff! I creep across to the zippered door and start to slowly unzip it. The rustling stops. I stop zipping. The rustling starts again. Very, very slowly I start unzipping again, until I can see outside. Glowing in the moonlight are two yellow eyes. That's no person, unless they are a zombie!!!!

As my eyes adjust to the light, I can see the eyes are attached to a small furry animal with a long curled tail. The eyes stop staring at me and the creature returns to eating the bread on the table. I decide to go out for a closer look (I know this is incredibly brave!). I'm pretty sure it's a possum and they are harmless, so I feel fairly safe. I walk right up to the end of the table…really close to it…and it still keeps eating, totally ignoring me.

Finally it finishes the bread (no toast for breakfast), gives me one last look with those big eyes and jumps off the table and wobbles into the nearby bushes.

I turn to go back to the tent. I scream! I scream again!! Eye to eye staring at me is a giant fur covered creature. As I open my mouth for a third scream, the creature turns and hops away. Uncle Jim appears at my shoulder, followed closely by my Dad. "Don't worry mate, it's just a kangaroo," says Uncle Jim, "back to bed everyone," he continues with a smile.

Wednesday

As the sun peeps over the horizon in the early dawn, Mrs. Bossy's whistle blasts me wide-awake. "Let's go, time to get up everyone!" she yells, scaring all the little animals within a mile of the camp. I scramble about in our tent in the gloom, trying to find my suitcase so I can change my clothes. After five minutes of searching through the mess in our tent, I realize that my suitcase must still be in the car (where the bread should be ☺). I search both cars…no suitcase!

I tell Mom I think my suitcase got left behind at the unit in Sydney. "Don't worry sweetie, after our walk I'll call the unit managers and see if your suitcase is still there," says Mom, while Mrs. Bossy slowly shakes her head.

I am desperate to change my clothes! I wore the clothes I have on now all yesterday and last night and they are starting to smell! But I just smile and thank her.

Mrs. Bossy sets a cracking pace and booms at us to "keep up" as we have to be back by 7:30 am to have breakfast. Breakfast is a bowl of cereal, so I don't know what the time deadline is all about. I suppose that is why I gave her the nickname of Mrs. Bossy.

We get back from the bushwalk. It is really hot here and walking so quickly has made me sweat all over my clothes.

Mom phones the holiday unit manager while we are eating. She walks over smiling and gives me the good news…my suitcase was left on the front lawn of the units. Then comes the bad news…"and the lovely man is going to keep it safe for you until we return to Sydney."

Silence. I try to process what she has just said.

"Mom, I CAN'T wear the same clothes for the whole holiday!" I beg.

"It's okay Maddi, there is a shop at Brooms Head," Mrs. Bossy calls out.

I feel so relieved, "I'm so glad there are some fashion shops at Brooms Head."

"Not shops Maddi, there is only one shop, it sells everything from petrol, food, tools, books and clothes," Mrs. Bossy replies with a smile.

Brains and Jack both have a little chuckle at that too. If I was a fan of those silly superhero movies, I'd say, "My spider senses are tingling," but obviously I'm too cool for that.

Uncle Jim drives Mom and I into Brooms Head. It's a lovely place, nice beach, nice camping ground, nice petrol station, nice shop. Yes...that's right, shop, not shops. Mrs. Bossy is right, it does have everything, food, takeaways, postcards, fishing gear, surfing stuff and even clothes. There is a lovely collection of clothes that you can choose from, you can have bright orange tie-dye shirts and matching shorts or bright yellow tie-dye shirts and matching shorts. In my real life I would never wear these clothes, but they are better than nothing. Mom buys me the orange and yellow outfits. I change into the orange clothes in the change room (behind a shower curtain at the back of the shop). When I come out, Mom gushes, "You look so gorgeous Madonna, I can remember wearing clothes like that when I was young." It is reassuring to know that my clothes were cool...in the 1980's!

When we arrive back at the campgrounds, my new outfit brings happiness to all. Everyone has a good laugh at me! I just smile. We spend the rest of the day swimming and lazing around at the beach, it's a great day.

That night I wake up desperately needing to go to the toilet. Everyone else is fast asleep and it is pitch black outside. I fumble around in the dark tent, trying to find a torch. I don't really want to walk to the toilet in the dark on my own. I try to make a bit of noise so that Brains will wake up and come with me. People with big brains must go into a very deep sleep…because she doesn't even budge when I crawl across her feet.

Finally I find the torch and *accidentally* shine it on Jack's face. Not surprisingly he wakes up. ☺ After a bit of begging, Jack reluctantly agrees to accompany me to the toilets.

A thick cloud cover is blocking out the moon. It is so totally dark, apart from the narrow band of light coming from the torch. One torch, two people – didn't really think that through! If I take the torch into the toilet, Jack will be outside in the dark all alone. There was NO WAY I was going into that pit toilet by myself in the dark.

I'm beginning to really like Jack; he actually volunteered to stand outside in the dark while I take the torch into the toilet with me. His last whispered instructions to me are to look after the torch; it is his Dad's super torch with a thousand different gadgets on it (I think that is a bit of an exaggeration). Jack told me it is only in our tent because he had borrowed it without asking.

The door creaks open and all I can see is what's in the small circle of light from the torch. For such a "super torch" it doesn't even give that much light. But there's enough light for me to see the spider webs hanging from the ceiling, some type of big black bug scuttling across the floor and a huge moth that starts fluttering madly around the light from the torch. Creepy! It's like I have stumbled onto the set of a horror movie!

After checking the seat for spiders and with the smell reminding me NOT to look down, I sit down and start to do what I have to do. It's then I hear a noise, a dry scratching type of sound. A quick flash of the torch reveals that I am alone in the toilet, except for spiders, moths and a bug. The noise keeps happening, so I rush to finish…when I realize that the noise seems to be coming from the toilet itself. I'm finally ready to leave when I decide to break Jack's rule of *Don't Look Down* to see what is making that noise. As I shine the light down into the pit, I see a pair of slit like eyes looking up at me. Just as my brain realizes what is looking up at me, a huge snake raises it's head and hisses. At the same time, the giant moth in an effort to get to the torch light, crashes into my hand holding the torch. I scream and drop the torch into the pit.

My new favorite cousin, Jack, races into the toilet shouting, "What's wrong!" I just point; it is as though I have lost the ability to speak. He comes in and stands beside me and we peer into the pit. The torch is working and its light is shining on the snake as it slowly moves towards the torch. The snake makes a sudden strike at the torch, grabbing it and swallowing it whole. The toilet is plunged into inky blackness. Both Jack and I scream, bolt from the room and run all the way back to the tent. As we climb into our sleeping bags, Jack whispers, "Dad must never know we lost his torch."

Thursday

In the morning I awake to the sound of a diesel engine rumbling away. The ranger is running a generator to power his tools as he does some maintenance on the toilet building.

My two cousins have already woken up and left the tent. I stumble outside in my yellow tie-dye outfit to see everyone standing around a table. I hear Uncle Jim saying, "I'm sure I left my torch right here on the table." Jack and I exchange worried and very guilty looks. I feel terrible and want to confess, but I promised Jack and he is keeping a very close eye on me.

We have just finished breakfast when the ranger wanders over and says, "You folks might want to come and have a look at this." As we walk over to the area in front of the pit toilet, Jack gives me a worried look. "Now we are in deep trouble," he whispers.

The ranger stops and points to a giant snake lying dead on the ground. "I pulled it out of the pit toilet," he says. It was disgusting, it was covered in "you know what"! He hosed it off and pointed to a lump, "Look at this," he said. "I'm guessing it is something it swallowed and eventually choked on...probably a large bush rat or something," he explains. Jack and I look at each other.

The ranger tells us he is going to cut it open, as he is curious to see what the snake had caught. It is pretty gross when he starts to cut into the snake, I want to look away, but I can't, I have to know.

The ranger gasps with surprise when Uncle Jim's torch is revealed as the mystery lump. Surprisingly Uncle Jim seems quite happy, "Look it is still working." He explains to the ranger how he had left his torch on the table; they agree that the snake must have taken it from there before crawling into the pit. The ranger hands back the torch to Uncle Jim, who gives it a quick wipe with a cloth.

I KNOW that Jack and I will NEVER touch that torch again, not ever!!!!!

We spend the morning kayaking in the little creek. It has beautiful, crystal clear water with little fish swimming around. The adults tried fishing but secretly I was happy when they didn't catch anything. Those little fish are so cute and adorable.

My cousins and I are getting on really well. We all paddle the kayak up the creek, while our parents set up for a picnic lunch. Even Mrs. Bossy seems happy today and she isn't bossing everyone around! Brains, Jack and I sit in some shallow water telling funny stories, when I decide to go for a swim to the middle of the creek. I lazily float on my back, watching the soft white clouds float past in the bright blue sky.

Suddenly my peaceful drifting is disturbed, when I hear the sound of a large splash from the other side of the creek. I turn lazily to look…and jerk upright rapidly. A large gray crocodile is swimming towards me! In a panicked flurry of arms, I explode into action and head towards the sandbank where Brains and Jack are sitting in the shallow water. I swim so fast that if I had been in the Olympics…I'm sure I would have won a gold medal! In between my frantic strokes I try to scream a warning to my cousins.

Yes, that's me…Maddi the hero. I can hear the news report now – "Maddi Bull is a true hero, despite being about to be torn

*apart from a savage crocodile...this young brave girl unselfishly
used some of her last breaths on Earth to warn her cousins."*

Unfortunately my warnings sound more like panicked
screams. It isn't until I reach the shallows and turn my
swimming into running that I'm able to finally get out some
clear intelligible words, "Run, Run, Crocodile!"

I am almost on the bank of the creek when I see my parents
and Uncle and Aunty looking down into the creek. How
horrible...I think, for my parents to see their only daughter
disappear into the jaws of a monster.

But then I hear laughter coming from the group of adults.
Soon Brains and Jack join in the laughter too. Maybe they are
just relieved that I am almost safe. I just keep running and
throw myself into Dad's arms...still screaming.

Uncle Jim manages to stop his laughter long enough to gasp
out, "That's not a crocodile, that's just a goanna." "Don't
worry Maddi, it won't hurt you, it is just a large lizard," he
says still smiling.

The goanna - formerly knows as crocodile, looks at us, then
it runs straight past. It now looks a lot smaller than it did in
the water. It runs up a tree trunk and hides amongst the
leaves. "Maddi," continues Uncle Jim, "we only have
crocodiles in Northern Australia, thousands of miles away
from here."

Friday

Today we leave Sandy River National Park and head to Yambucca Heads (who makes up these weird names!!!) moving on to civilization as Dad calls it. It takes an hour to pack up the tents and another hour making sure not one tiny molecule of dirt or sand ends up in Uncle Jim's car. We have to vacuum everything before it goes in the car. Not even Mrs. Bossy can get him to hurry up.

Finally we set off, this time I'm traveling with Mom and Dad!!! As I sit in the back in my matching tie-dye orange outfit, I ask the most important question.

"Are there any clothes shops in Yambucca Heads?" Neither of my parents know, so I'll just have to live in hope.

About two hours later we arrive in Yambucca Heads. As we cruise up the one main street, one thing is clear, this is not civilization, as we know it. Yambucca is a little fishing and surfing town with lots of fishing boats, a very old movie cinema which appears to only show old surfing movies and three shops with surfboards for sale out the front. The trendy, fully stocked fashion shop appears to exist only in my hopeful mind.

We find the campground we are staying at. It is at the end of the main (or should I say – only street). For the first three days we will be staying here and then Dad gets his luxury, another three days in a house before we fly home. We take the rest of the day setting up our tents. It is a lot different to Sandy River. Here there are heaps of tents crammed in together and instead of the peaceful sounds of nature…all we can hear is the sounds of other campers. The best news is that there is a REAL toilet and hot showers!

Saturday

When Mrs. Bossy's whistle goes off in the morning it doesn't worry me, I've been awake for ages. The sound of tent zips being opened and shut and lots of too loud voices from the little children (who seem to be overrunning this campground) woke me at sunrise.

After breakfast, Mrs. Bossy announces that we kids should spend the day at the campground's Kids' Club, while the adults have some relaxation time.

Miss Jane is the lady in charge of the Kids' Club and she is really nice, but she talks to everyone like they are 4 years old. "Oh Maddi, what a lovely name," she gushes, "and darling what cute little dimples you have." How embarrassing! Then she picks on Jack, "And you Jack, tell me darling, are you the little man of the family?" Jack's face went bright red. Brains gives her a look that says: Don't Talk To Me!

The other children attending the Kids' Club are all playing in an undercover area. There are about 20 kids and it is very clear that Brains and I are the oldest.

The first hour passes at the speed of a wounded snail! Yes, we make macaroni necklaces! Miss Jane raves about Brain's necklace, she makes her stand up and show everyone. Brains looks like she wants aliens to abduct her. There is something sweet about Miss Jane though. She has a good heart and is trying her best to give us a good time. She calls everyone "darling", in fact she uses darling in each and every sentence that comes from her sweet mouth. So her new name is going to be Miss Darling.

The second hour involves some chalk drawings on the

concrete walkway and some face painting. Miss Darling lets Brains and I paint the little kids. Brains paints her brother as the devil, he wants to be Superman, so he isn't happy when he looks in the mirror. Brains can't stop laughing, she has tears rolling down her face and she starts snorting

We have a BBQ lunch. Over our burnt sausages, Brains and I shared our imaginings of how to escape Kids' Club.

Then Miss Darling announces that after lunch we are playing volleyball. Brains and I groan, apparently like me, Brains is no sporting legend. But when we see the volleyball court our faces light up. We strap on our kneepads and race to make sure we are on the same side.

Why so suddenly enthusiastic you may ask? The net only comes up to our shoulders. After two games where we dominate, with great spikes and lots of high fives (we feel invincible, like superheroes), Miss Darling pulls us off the court to let the little kids have a fair game.

We end the Kids' Club session with a movie, I've already seen it, so I help Miss Darling to clean up. Brains has instant popularity status after the volleyball game and is sitting surrounded by little kids. They love her! Finally Mom collects us and as we walk back to our tent site I notice both Brains and Jack scratching their heads...a lot!

The next morning Brain's hair is looking like she has dreadlocks and Jack's is even messier than usual. Both are still scratching at their heads madly. Then Mrs. Bossy utters those fearful words, "I think you've got headlice."

Uncle Jim says, "Don't worry, I can get rid of them, into the tent you two."

Mon and Dad commence a whispered conversation with Mrs. Bossy. Meanwhile I hear a buzzing sound coming from the tent. When Jack and Brains emerge I realize what Uncle Jim's headlice remedy is...he has shaved Jack's hair down to a stubble and Brains hair isn't much longer.

Then Uncle Jim says, "Have you got them too Maddi, come over here and I'll check your hair."

That's when Mom reminds me how much I love her, as she says, "No Jim, it's okay, I'll check Maddi's hair myself." Fortunately I have no headlice. Mom quietly reassures me that even if I did, she wouldn't allow Uncle Jim to shave my head.

Brains, Jack and I go for a walk along the river. I tell Brains how sorry I feel for her. She is really quite cool about it and tells me it is the third time she has had the same headlice treatment. "Don't worry Maddi, it will grow back," she says shrugging her shoulders.

As we walk past the playground near the beach, I notice some of the local kids staring at us. I'm wearing my tie-dye clothes today and with Brain's shaven hair, we do stand out. Rudely they call out, "Hey baldy, what's with your friend's weird outfit!" I whisper to Brains to just ignore them, while little Jack slinks between us. As we continue to walk past, the insults keep flying.

Then I get one of my brilliant ideas. In my worst fake French accent I say to the girl, "You do not understand, we have come direct from Paris. I point at Brains, "She is a famous French teen model, that is the hottest hairstyle in Paris right now and this tie dye print cost $100 and everyone over there is wearing them. I know your little town is a bit isolated but I would have thought even here you'd have heard of the latest styles." Before the locals even get a chance to reply…Brains bursts out with a torrent of French and extravagant gestures. We keep walking leaving the local kids looking confused in our wake.

The three of us burst out laughing. Brains says, "That was so funny Maddi!" I ask her how come she speaks French so well. Her reply is typical, "I told you I'm a genius Maddi. I speak French, Spanish and Mandarin." We spend the rest of the day at the beach, holidays are so wonderful.

That night we head out for dinner at the local Chinese restaurant. It looks really fancy and sits on top of the one hill in Yambucca Heads. The restaurant is really crowded but we get a table in about the middle of the restaurant. All the dishes have difficult to pronounce Chinese names. So it's quite funny when Mrs. Bossy decides she will order for all of us. In her loud voice she struggles with the unusual words as she orders, from the look on the face of the waiter, he doesn't understand most of what she is trying to say. The first waiter calls a second waiter over when Mrs. Bossy tries to order a second time. She does just as bad a job at pronouncing the words…saying them slower and louder. The two waiters are very polite but you can see they are trying very hard not to laugh.

Just when it's looking like everyone at our table is going to die either of embarrassment or starvation, Brains saves the day. She bursts into some rapid fire Chinese, quickly ordering our meals. I get the feeling she might have added a little joke about her Mom at the end, as both waiters had a little chuckle and a quick glance at Mrs. Bossy.

The meals are beautiful and we all enjoy them. My favorite is a seafood dish with prawns, fish and even whole tiny little octopuses. Brains is enjoying showing off her language skills and keeps having conversations with the waiters in Chinese as they bring out the different dishes.

One of the waiters is very young, only about our age. I'm guessing his family owns the restaurant. Brains seems to enjoy practicing her language skills on this boy. Every time he comes over to our table he talks to Brains…but keeps glaring at me. I'm sure he's looking at me! After a while I have to say something to Brains, "That boy keeps staring at me," I whisper. "I know," she replies, "I think he might like you." My face goes instantly red, but even redder when Brains tells me she's going to ask him what he is looking at me for! "No!" I whisper shout (didn't you know you could shout and whisper at the same time, you learn something everyday). Brains ignores me and bursts into Chinese and the boy answers…looking at me again.

When he has left I ask what he said, Brains answers, "He said you have beautiful eyes."

My face goes into full meltdown mode, I almost slide under the table. As everyone has finished their meals we are walking out to the front of the restaurant while Dad and Mrs. Bossy pay the bill. Suddenly I hear a voice calling, "Miss, miss, please wait." I turn to see the young waiter hurrying towards me. He stops in front of me and smiles. Then he reaches a hand out towards my face. My brain is racing, what is he doing? His fingers gently pull a tiny little octopus (from my seafood meal) out of my hair. "Your friend told me you were keeping this for a late night snack, but I think she was just playing a trick on you," he explained. I mumble an embarrassed thanks and rush after Brains. She was nearly crying she is laughing so much. "Now that I think about it," she says, "Maybe it was the octopus' eyes that he thought were beautiful."

Monday

I wake up the next morning in a very happy mood, last night was our last night in the tent. Today we move into Dad's style accommodation, an actual house that Dad has rented for us. It's called the 'Blue House', it turns out it's just down the road from the camping ground. When we first see it we feel pretty disappointed, it's a dump.

Dad looks pretty dejected too, as he booked it, but when we go inside all our faces light up. It's fantastic! It's cool. It's been completely renovated and is very modern and perfectly clean.

The best part is that the kids have a totally separate area with a TV, bunk beds and a heap of board games. The board games didn't feel as exciting though, after Brains beat me at scrabble three times in a row by about one hundred points using words that I couldn't even spell. I didn't even know what they meant, but sure enough, every one of them was in the dictionary.

When we explore the house we discover an unusual design feature, the downstairs definitely hasn't been renovated. An old creaky dark stairway leads down to the underneath, we are talking creepy, serious horror movie creeps.

The floor was plain concrete, the walls were also rough concrete and the ceiling was just open rafters. The lights were just bare bulbs. In the middle of this dusty dim dungeon like room, sat a white shiny bath on claw feet with rusty taps coming up from the floor. I just stare at the bath and think, 'No way am I sitting down here in that,' Brains says, "How cool! I can't wait to have a bath down here!" Jack just holds my hand and shakes his head.

So is born my idea of revenge on Brains for the waiter joke. That night Brains collects her toiletries and heads down stairs to enjoy her bath. I try to enlist Jack's help but when I combine down stairs and dark in one sentence he runs and hides under his blanket on his bed.

Ah well, looks like this will be a solo mission for Maddi the brave. Fortunately for me the light switch for the whole downstairs area is at the bottom of the stairway and the stairway is enclosed, so Brains can't see me from the bath. I slowly make my way down the stairs, wincing at each creak as my feet go from one step to the next. I needn't worry about Brains hearing me as she is singing. The term singing covers a wide range of sound. Let's just say, American Idol contestants…you have nothing to fear from Brains!

I'm just reaching toward the light switch when I hear the door at the top of the stairway swing and close with a bang. It cuts out the light from upstairs and now the stairway is quite dark and I can just see the light switch. The bang of the door cuts through Brains singing, she stops, obviously listening, wondering what the noise is. Perfect, I can feel her tension building. "Who's there?" she calls out in a nervous voice.

That's when I strike…reaching out and hit the light switch, plunging the entire room and stairway into complete darkness. Brains screams, I scream louder and in panic can't find the light switch. As I am fumbling around trying to find the lights, Brains comes flying round the corner and smashes into me. We both scream again in unison as we fall in a heap on the floor.

Suddenly the stairway is flooded in light as Mrs. Bossy appears at the top of the stairs. "What on Earth are you girls doing?" she booms.

In the light…our fear evaporates and we both start laughing as Brains realizes what I was up to. We are still chuckling over dinner although I'm not sure Mrs. Bossy finds it as funny as we do.

Tuesday

Brains, Jack and I are walking down to the beach when we hear someone yelling. We turn around to see the girl who was harassing us the other day, rushing towards us. "Oh no," I groan. While Jack whispers, "Lets just run!"

"No," Brains says, "Check her out."

"Bonjour!" the girl calls out with a big smile on her face. I have to bite down hard on my tongue to stop from laughing. She has cut her hair very short and is wearing a tie-dye top (obviously home made because they it is not tie-dyed very well). She even put has tie-dye material on her boots. I break out my terrible French accent again and say, "Oh wonderful! You are the height of fashion now! I bet everyone in town is looking at you!"

Brains starts speaking French again, with a couple of sentences which make no sense to anyone else. As we go our separate ways everyone has a smile on their face.

Once we are far enough away so she can't hear us, Brains says, "Maddi let that be a lesson to you, never be a slave to fashion." I glance down at my own tie-dye outfit and think no one can ever accuse me of being fashionable.

That night I look everywhere trying to find my book, but it's nowhere to be seen. I'm about to give up when Jack whispers to me, "I think Jenny hid it downstairs." I thank Jack for the tip off and head down the stairway to collect my book. I get to the bottom and discover my book sitting on the edge of the bathtub. That should have been enough warning for me. I hear the door at the top of the stairs bang shut and the sound of the bolt sliding across to lock it. I feel a shiver run up my spine at the thought of being locked up in this scary room. But then I remember that there are two other doors down here, one that goes out into the backyard through a little laundry. I rush over to the one leading to the side yard and am about to open it when I hear voices outside. Yes, of course, Brains and Jack have realized I'll try to escape through the closest door. They'll be waiting there to scare me when I come out. Except I'm way too smart for them, I creep away from the side door and head towards the door that heads to the backyard. I'll go out the back door creep around to the side door where they're obviously waiting for me and scare them first.

The locking bolt on the side door is very rusty and even though I try very hard, it still makes quite a loud noise as I work it loose. I stay still for a moment, hoping that no one hears me unlocking the door. The only thing I can hear is my own heartbeat and breathing. I smile in anticipation of scaring my cousins as I swing open the door. Suddenly I jump back in fright as a pair of hands appear in front of my face and clap twice loudly. I scream and fall back through the door landing on my bottom.

Brains steps through the door laughing hysterically, "Got you," she gasps between laughs. We walk up the stairs arm in arm…like the best friends we have become. Jack scrambles up behind us, his big smile reflecting his joy in helping to trick me.

Thursday

Our final day, we all feel pretty sad as we pack up and leave the little blue house and Yambucca heads. I have fun with my cousins on the trip back to Sydney but knowing that soon we will have to say goodbye puts a damper on the trip. Before you know it we are at the airport, after a detour to pick up my suitcase that was left at the units. A quick change in the airport toilets sees me back in normal clothes at last. We say our sad farewells to our relatives, with promises from them to visit us next year.

Boarding the plane I look out for Miss Perfect, but she is nowhere to be seen. The trip home seems quicker, probably because I sleep most of the way. I didn't even notice Dad's snoring or Mom's singing.

Monday Morning

My first day back at school today, I've missed two weeks and dread to think of how much work I have to catch up.

A bigger shock is when I walk into class and discover a new girl sitting next to my very good friend, Richard…also know as: Mr. Tall Dark and Handsome. I sit next to my other friend Gretel. After a welcome hug and a few "I missed you so much"…I get straight to the point. "WHO IS THAT next to Mr. TDH?"

Gretel asks me, "Do you mean the tall slim beautiful girl with the long blonde hair?"

"Of course I mean her," I reply gruffly. Gretel tells me she is a new girl at our school, Linda Douglas, she continues on by also telling me that she isn't very nice. "Why is she sitting next to Mr. TDH then?" I ask.

"Probably because she looks nice," replies Gretel with a weak smile. At lunch I get to meet Linda, when I go to say hi to Mr. TDH he seems happy to see me and I start to entertain him with my highly amusing stories from my holiday to Australia.

Then along comes Linda and interrupts us. "You must be the girl who was on holiday in Australia. Michelle isn't it?"

"No, my name is 'Maddi'."

Linda continues with, "Whatever, look at that hair, did you leave your brush back in Australia?" She smiles and pulls her sleek blonde hair away from her face. "Anyway Maddi, run along now, I need to speak to Richard about an assignment we are going to do together," says Linda as she drags Mr. TDH away by the arm.

After lunch I sit next to Gretel still fuming over Linda's treatment of me. "Don't worry about her Maddi, you should have seen her last week with our buddy class. Her little buddy messed up her perfect hair and Linda yelled at him and made the poor kid cry."

I can't help but watch her, she's mean and she's sitting next to Mr. TDH. That's when I notice that she seems to be scratching her head a lot, so much that her perfect hair isn't looking so perfect anymore. Suddenly it clicks. I ask Gretel who Linda's buddy was?

"Harry," she replies with a smirk on her face. Harry is also known as *Harry Headlice*. Harry is one of those unfortunate children who always seem to have a case of headlice. A wondrous plan hatches in my brain, while the rest of the class does math.

This is my plan:
Contact Brains and ask her to write two letters to Linda's parents
– a headlice notice from my school and a second letter explaining
the latest chemical free way to beat headlice - all the way from
Australia.

Follow Linda home so I know where she lives.

Put Brain's letters in her letterbox - addressed to her parents.

Okay, I felt like a stalker following her home, but a girl's got to do what a girl's got to do!

I phone Brains and she is excited to hear from me. "Oh Maddi, you are so naughty! Of course I will help you, give me an hour." With that she got straight to work. The email arrives in under an hour. I dress in dark clothes, put on a big floppy hat and casually walk to Linda's house and put the letters in their letter box.

Tuesday

The next day, the success of my plan is plain to see. Linda's long blonde hair is gone…replaced by very short hair. I guess that means no more mean comments about other girls' hair.

That night I email Brains thanking her for the two letters. It's great having a super smart cousin.

Now I just have to figure out how to get Linda moved from sitting next to Mr. TDH.

Thank you for reading
my book!
I hope you liked it.
If you did, can you please
leave me a review?
I really appreciate your
help.

 Maddi and Bill

Hi Almost Cool Girls,
Can you do me a HUGE favor?
Please leave a review.
5 stars means you liked the book.
Thank you so much!!!!

Some other books you will love…

Made in the USA
San Bernardino, CA
19 October 2016